W9-AZJ-404

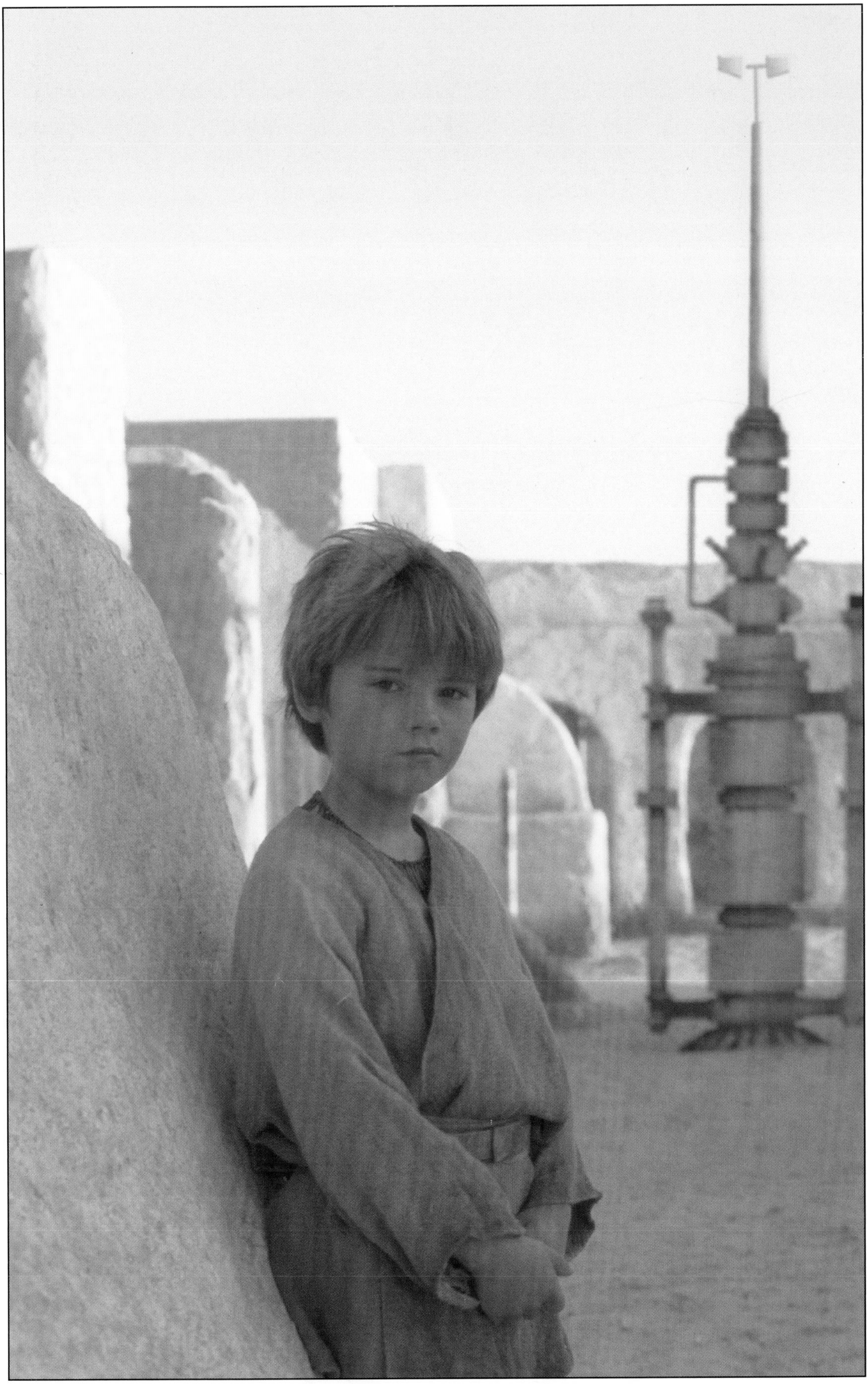

STAR WARS®

EPISODE I
THE PHANTOM MENACE™

VOLUME TWO

ADAPTED BY
HENRY GILROY

FROM AN ORIGINAL STORY BY
GEORGE LUCAS

PENCILS
RODOLFO DAMAGGIO

INKS
AL WILLIAMSON

COLORS
DAVE NESTELLE

COLOR SEPARATOR
HAROLD MACKINNON

LETTERS
STEVE DUTRO

COVER ART
HUGH FLEMING

DARK HORSE COMICS

VISIT US AT
www.abdopublishing.com

Reinforced library bound edition published in 2009 by Spotlight, a division of the ABDO Group, 8000 West 78th Street, Edina, Minnesota 55439. Spotlight produces high-quality reinforced library bound editions for schools and libraries. Published by agreement with Dark Horse Comics, Inc., and Lucasfilm Ltd.

Library of Congress Cataloging-in-Publication Data

Gilroy, Henry.
  Episode I : the phantom menace / story, George Lucas ; script, Henry Gilroy ; pencils, Rodolfo Damaggio ; inks, Al Williamson ; colors, Dave Nestelle ; letters, Steve Dutro. -- Reinforced library bound ed.
      p. cm. -- (Star Wars)
  ISBN 978-1-59961-608-7 (v.1) -- ISBN 978-1-59961-609-4 (v.2) -- ISBN 978-1-59961-610-0 (v.3) -- ISBN 978-1-59961-611-7 (v.4)
  1. Graphic novels. [1. Graphic novels.] I. Lucas, George, 1944- II. Damaggio, Rodolfo. III. Williamson, Al, 1931- IV. Nestelle, Dave. V. Dutro, Steve. VI. Star wars, episode I, the phantom menace (Motion picture) VII. Title.
  PZ7.7.G55Epi 2009
  [Fic]--dc22
                        2008038310

All Spotlight books have reinforced library bindings and are manufactured in the United States of America.

Episode I

THE PHANTOM MENACE

Volume 2

Two Jedi Knights, Qui-Gon Jinn and Obi-Wan Kenobi, have been sent by the Supreme Chancellor to negotiate a settlement between the Trade Federation and the planet of Naboo.

Prior to their planned meeting, the Knights discover the Trade Federation's army of droids waiting to invade Naboo and quickly leave with hopes of warning Queen Amidala and the Senate.

In the capital, the Jedi arrive just in time to assure the Queen can escape with them to plead the Naboo case before the Senate. Unfortunately, a failed hyperdrive forces their ship to make an emergency landing on the planet of Tatooine . . .

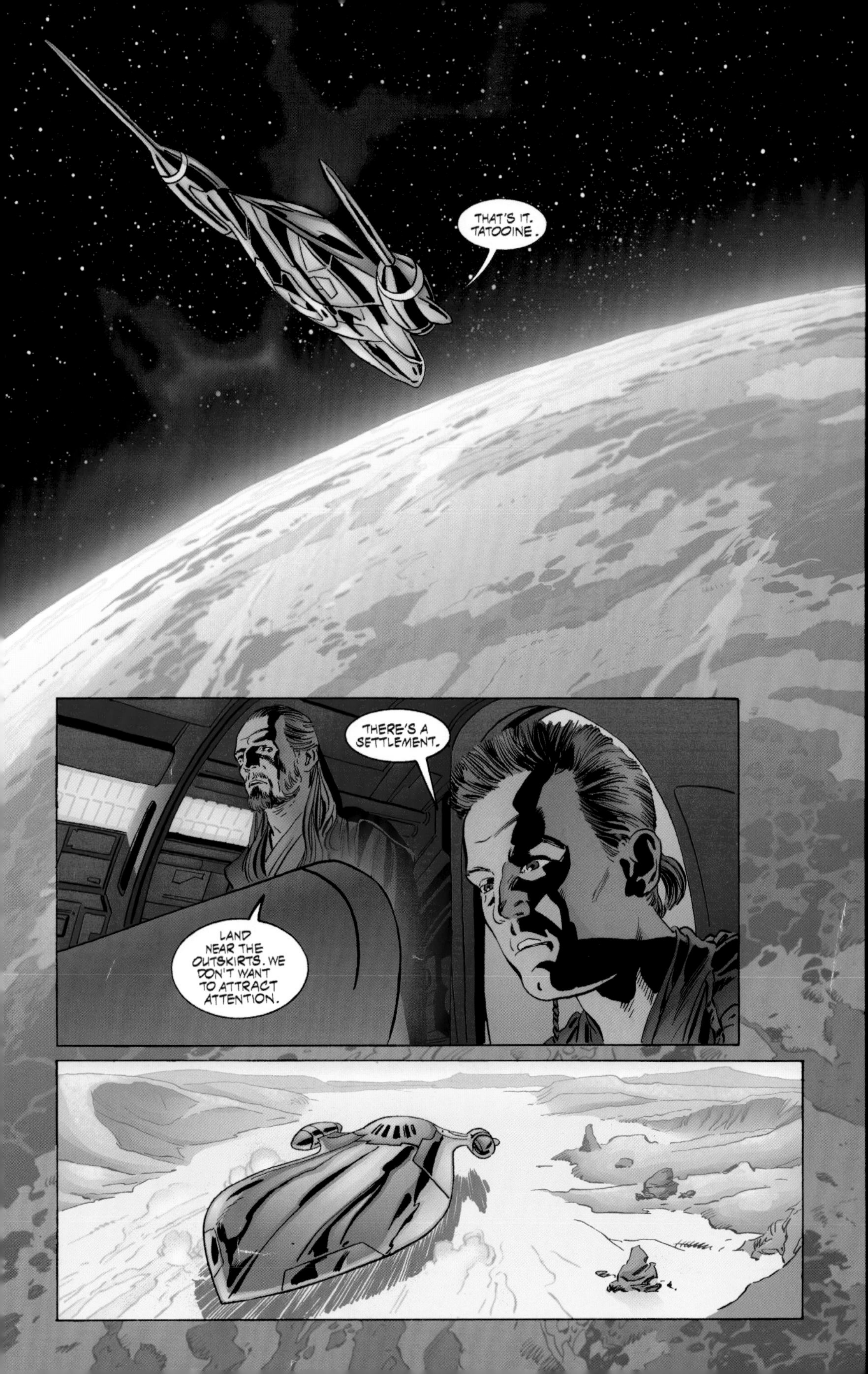
THAT'S IT. TATOOINE.
THERE'S A SETTLEMENT.
LAND NEAR THE OUTSKIRTS. WE DON'T WANT TO ATTRACT ATTENTION.

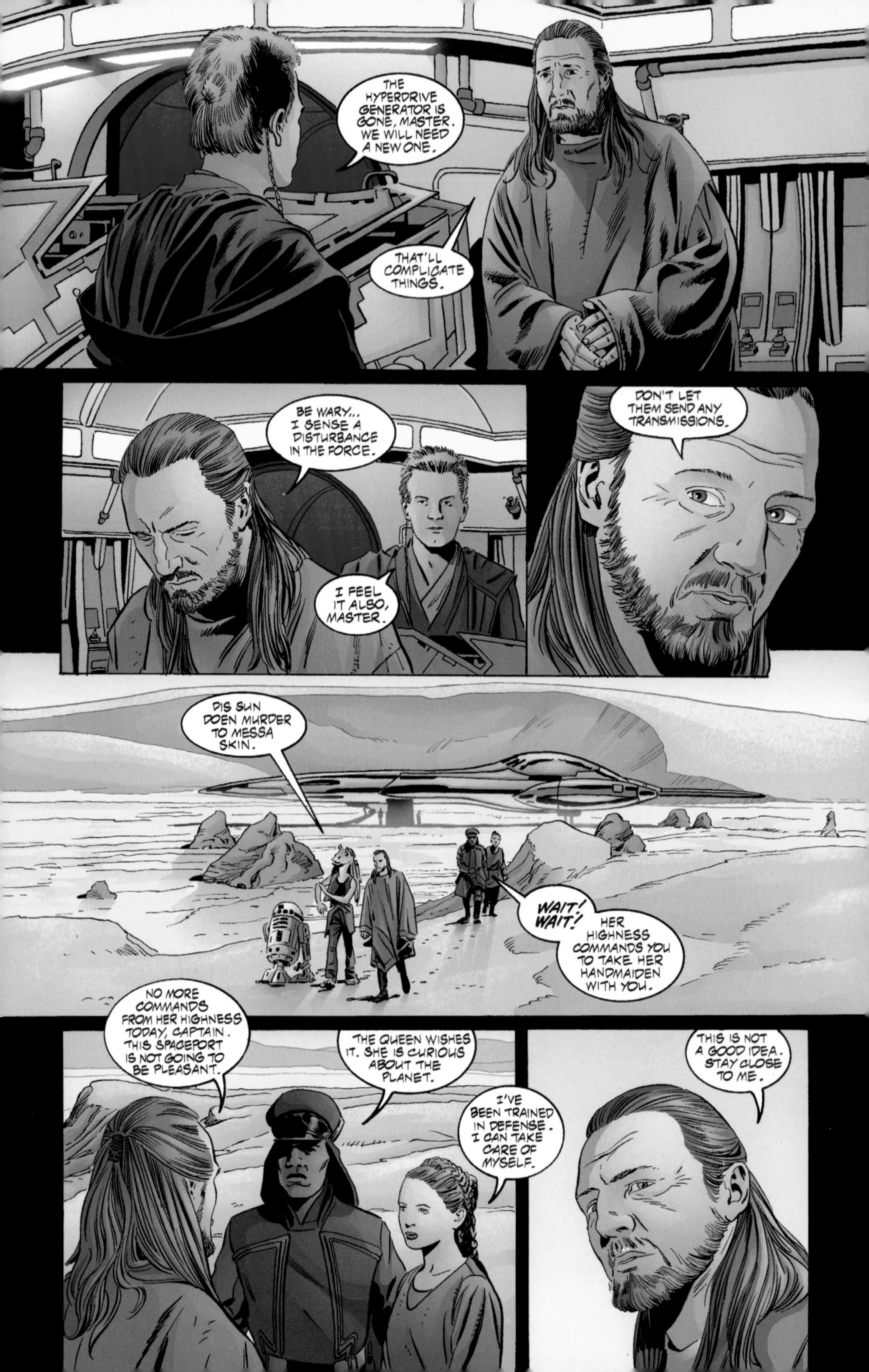
THE HYPERDRIVE GENERATOR IS GONE, MASTER. WE WILL NEED A NEW ONE.
THAT'LL COMPLICATE THINGS.
BE WARY... I SENSE A DISTURBANCE IN THE FORCE.
I FEEL IT ALSO, MASTER.
DON'T LET THEM SEND ANY TRANSMISSIONS.
DIS SUN DOEN MURDER TO MESSA SKIN.
WAIT! WAIT!
HER HIGHNESS COMMANDS YOU TO TAKE HER HANDMAIDEN WITH YOU.
NO MORE COMMANDS FROM HER HIGHNESS TODAY, CAPTAIN. THIS SPACEPORT IS NOT GOING TO BE PLEASANT.
THE QUEEN WISHES IT. SHE IS CURIOUS ABOUT THE PLANET.
I'VE BEEN TRAINED IN DEFENSE. I CAN TAKE CARE OF MYSELF.
THIS IS NOT A GOOD IDEA. STAY CLOSE TO ME.

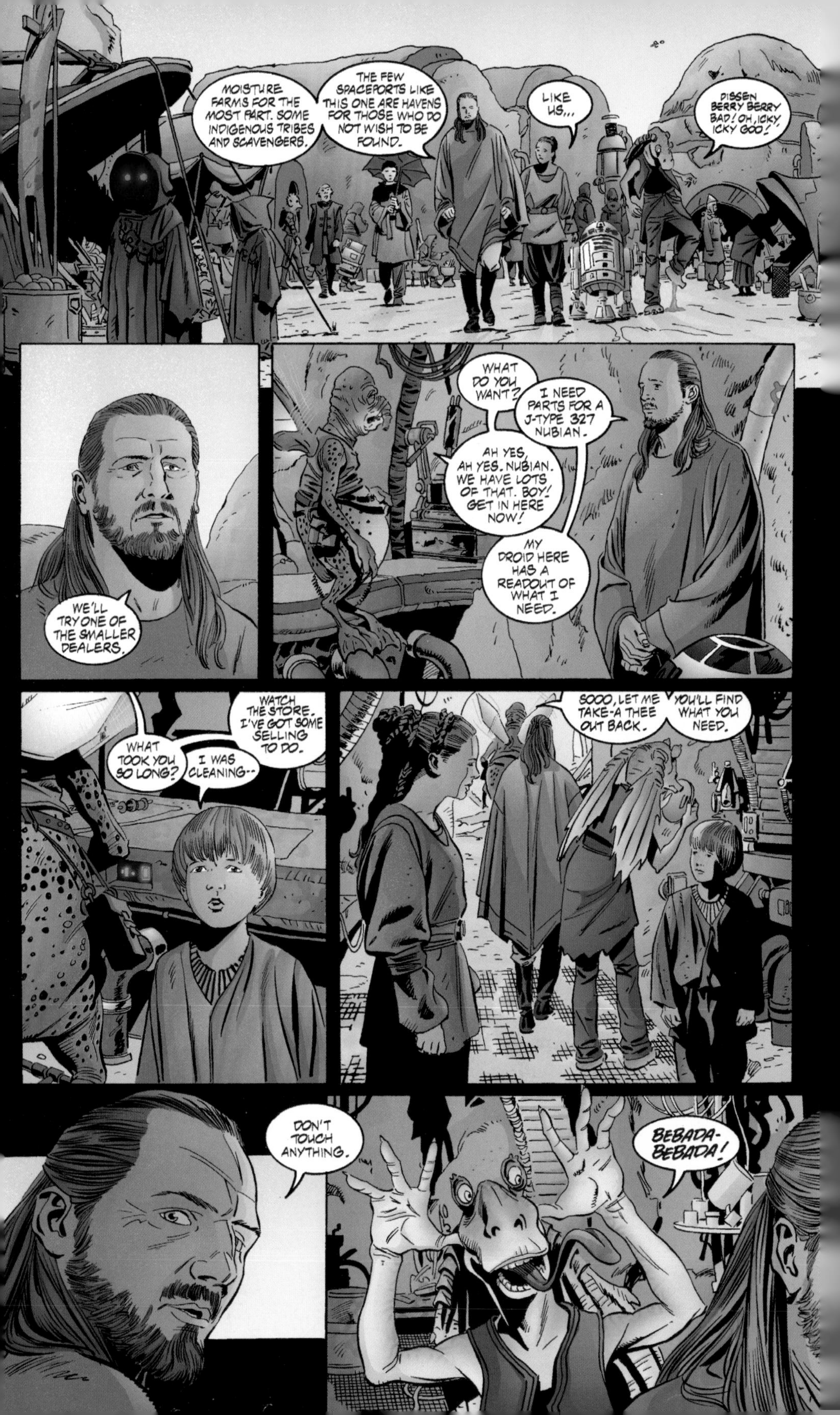
MOISTURE FARMS FOR THE MOST PART. SOME INDIGENOUS TRIBES AND SCAVENGERS.
THE FEW SPACEPORTS LIKE THIS ONE ARE HAVENS FOR THOSE WHO DO NOT WISH TO BE FOUND.
LIKE US...
DISSEN BERRY BERRY BAD! OH, ICKY, ICKY GOO!
WE'LL TRY ONE OF THE SMALLER DEALERS.
WHAT DO YOU WANT?
I NEED PARTS FOR A J-TYPE 327 NUBIAN.
AH YES, AH YES. NUBIAN. WE HAVE LOTS OF THAT. BOY! GET IN HERE NOW!
MY DROID HERE HAS A READOUT OF WHAT I NEED.
WHAT TOOK YOU SO LONG?
I WAS CLEANING--
WATCH THE STORE. I'VE GOT SOME SELLING TO DO.
SOOO, LET ME TAKE-A THEE OUT BACK.
YOU'LL FIND WHAT YOU NEED.
DON'T TOUCH ANYTHING.
BEBADA-BEBADA!

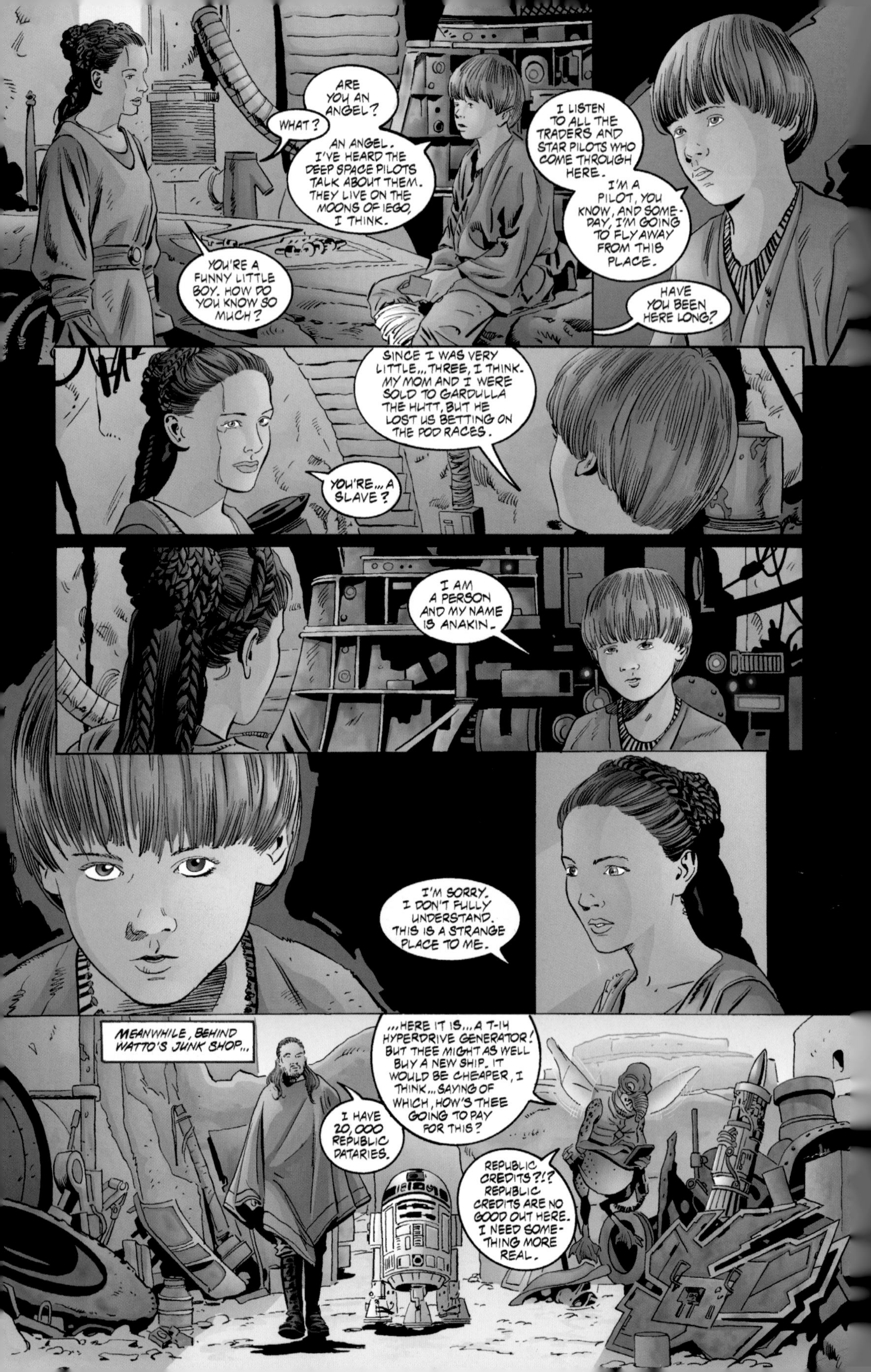
ARE YOU AN ANGEL?
WHAT?
AN ANGEL. I'VE HEARD THE DEEP SPACE PILOTS TALK ABOUT THEM. THEY LIVE ON THE MOONS OF IEGO, I THINK.
YOU'RE A FUNNY LITTLE BOY. HOW DO YOU KNOW SO MUCH?
I LISTEN TO ALL THE TRADERS AND STAR PILOTS WHO COME THROUGH HERE.
I'M A PILOT, YOU KNOW, AND SOMEDAY, I'M GOING TO FLY AWAY FROM THIS PLACE.
HAVE YOU BEEN HERE LONG?
SINCE I WAS VERY LITTLE... THREE, I THINK. MY MOM AND I WERE SOLD TO GARDULLA THE HUTT, BUT HE LOST US BETTING ON THE POD RACES.
YOU'RE... A SLAVE?
I AM A PERSON AND MY NAME IS ANAKIN.
I'M SORRY. I DON'T FULLY UNDERSTAND. THIS IS A STRANGE PLACE TO ME.
MEANWHILE, BEHIND WATTO'S JUNK SHOP...
...HERE IT IS... A T-14 HYPERDRIVE GENERATOR! BUT THEE MIGHT AS WELL BUY A NEW SHIP. IT WOULD BE CHEAPER, I THINK... SAYING OF WHICH, HOW'S THEE GOING TO PAY FOR THIS?
I HAVE 20,000 REPUBLIC DATARIES.
REPUBLIC CREDITS?!? REPUBLIC CREDITS ARE NO GOOD OUT HERE. I NEED SOMETHING MORE REAL.

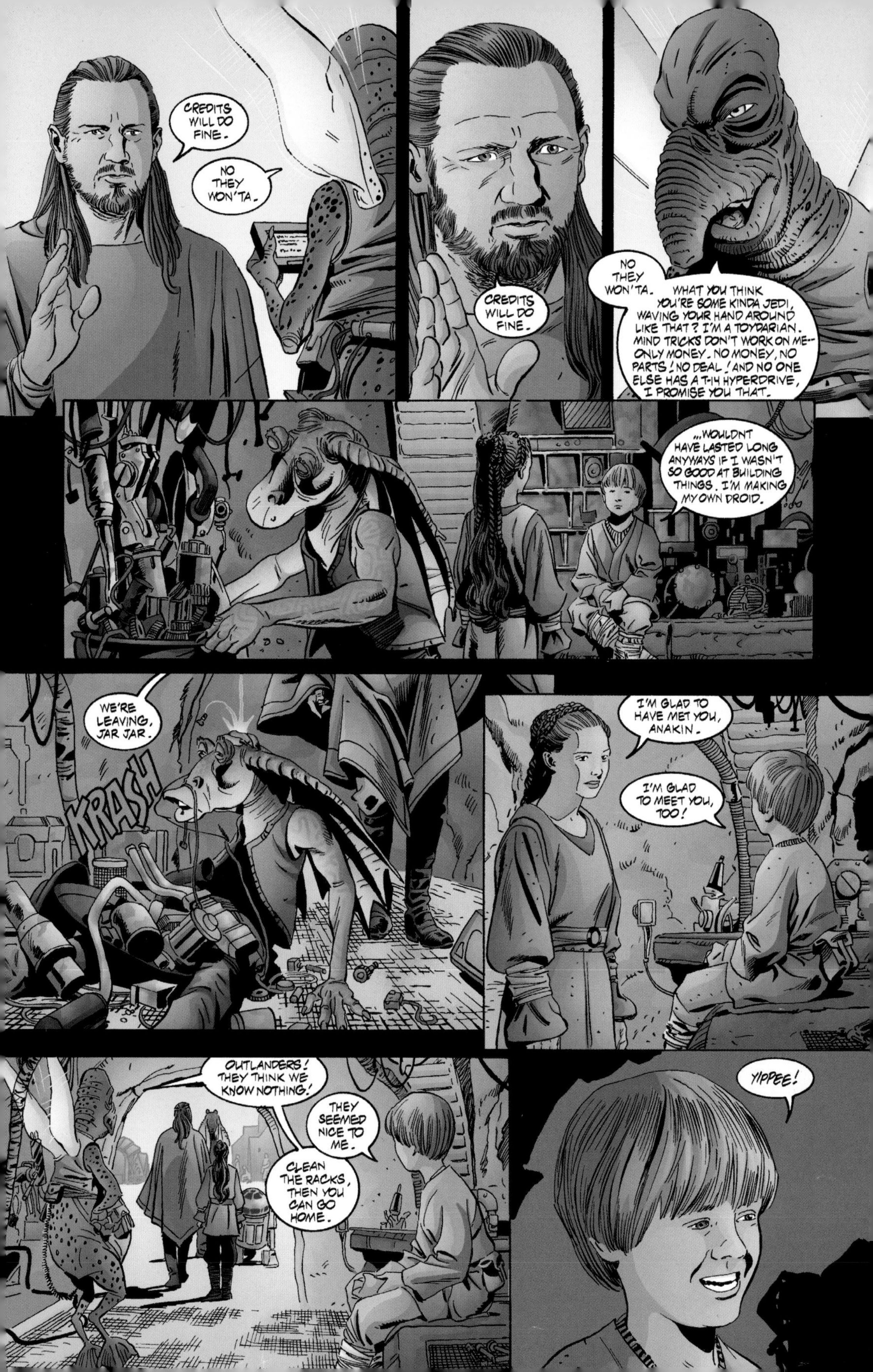
CREDITS WILL DO FINE.
NO THEY WON'TA.
CREDITS WILL DO FINE.
NO THEY WON'TA. WHAT YOU THINK YOU'RE SOME KINDA JEDI, WAVING YOUR HAND AROUND LIKE THAT? I'M A TOYDARIAN. MIND TRICKS DON'T WORK ON ME-- ONLY MONEY. NO MONEY, NO PARTS! NO DEAL! AND NO ONE ELSE HAS A T-14 HYPERDRIVE, I PROMISE YOU THAT.
...WOULDNT HAVE LASTED LONG ANYWAYS IF I WASN'T SO GOOD AT BUILDING THINGS. I'M MAKING MY OWN DROID.
WE'RE LEAVING, JAR JAR.
KRASH
I'M GLAD TO HAVE MET YOU, ANAKIN.
I'M GLAD TO MEET YOU, TOO!
OUTLANDERS! THEY THINK WE KNOW NOTHING!
THEY SEEMED NICE TO ME.
CLEAN THE RACKS, THEN YOU CAN GO HOME.
YIPPEE!

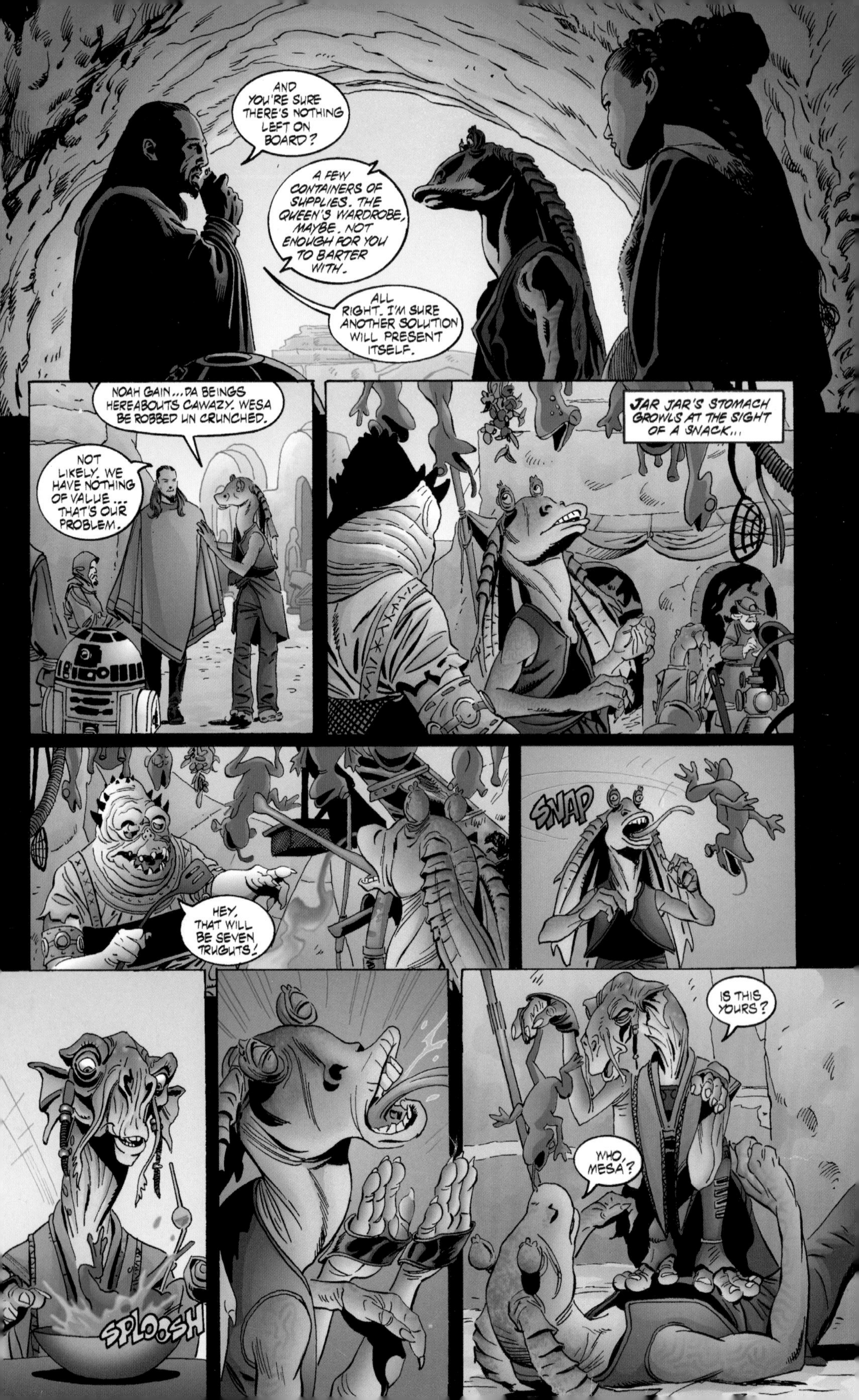
AND YOU'RE SURE THERE'S NOTHING LEFT ON BOARD?
A FEW CONTAINERS OF SUPPLIES. THE QUEEN'S WARDROBE, MAYBE. NOT ENOUGH FOR YOU TO BARTER WITH.
ALL RIGHT. I'M SURE ANOTHER SOLUTION WILL PRESENT ITSELF.
NOAH GAIN... DA BEINGS HEREABOUTS CAWAZY. WESA BE ROBBED UN CRUNCHED.
NOT LIKELY. WE HAVE NOTHING OF VALUE... THAT'S OUR PROBLEM.
JAR JAR'S STOMACH GROWLS AT THE SIGHT OF A SNACK...
HEY, THAT WILL BE SEVEN TRUGUTS!
SNAP
SPLOOSH
IS THIS YOURS?
WHO, MESA?

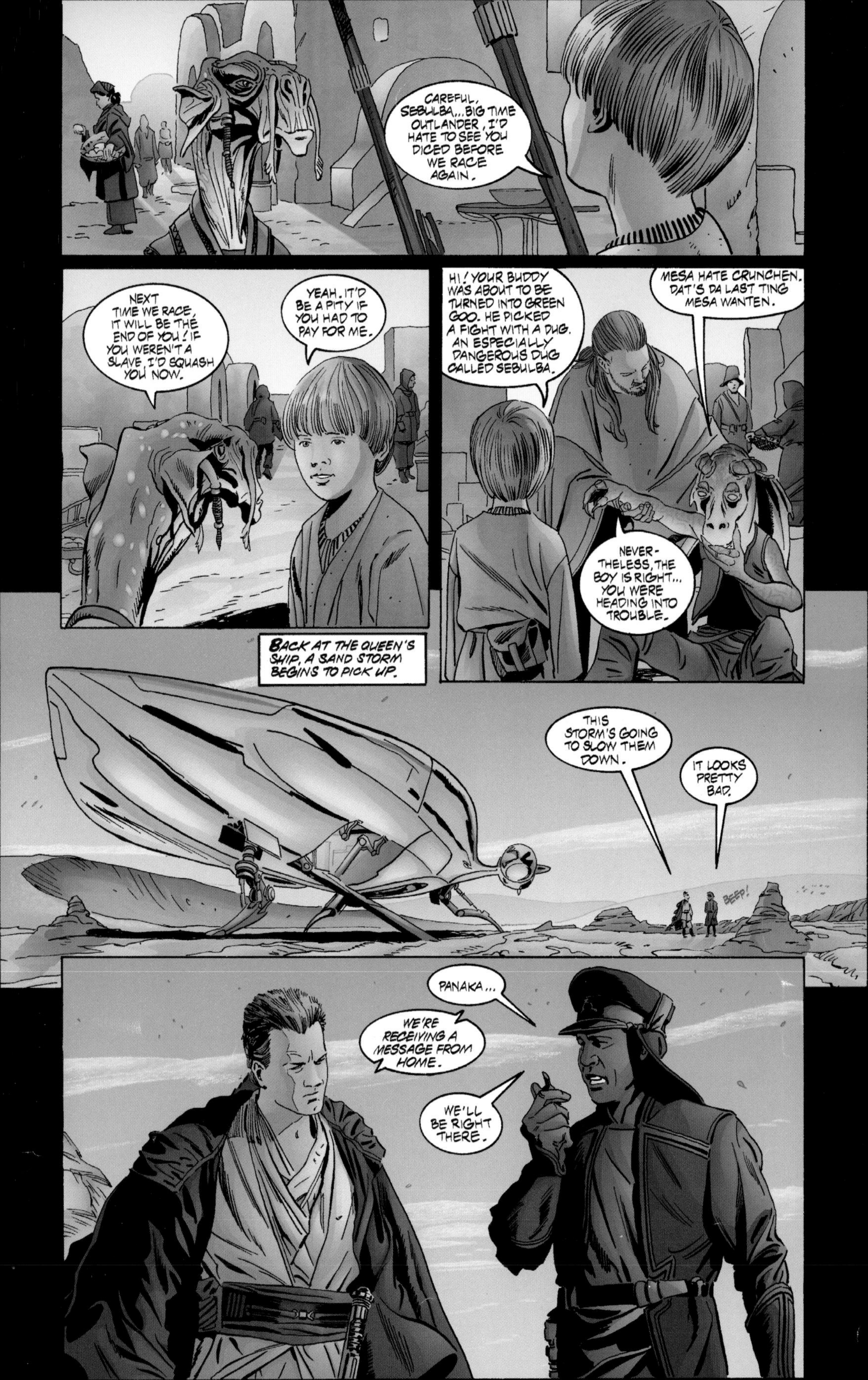
CAREFUL, SEBULBA... BIG TIME OUTLANDER, I'D HATE TO SEE YOU DICED BEFORE WE RACE AGAIN.
NEXT TIME WE RACE, IT WILL BE THE END OF YOU! IF YOU WEREN'T A SLAVE, I'D SQUASH YOU NOW.
YEAH. IT'D BE A PITY IF YOU HAD TO PAY FOR ME.
HI! YOUR BUDDY WAS ABOUT TO BE TURNED INTO GREEN GOO. HE PICKED A FIGHT WITH A DUG. AN ESPECIALLY DANGEROUS DUG CALLED SEBULBA.
MESA HATE CRUNCHEN. DAT'S DA LAST TING MESA WANTEN.
NEVER-THELESS, THE BOY IS RIGHT... YOU WERE HEADING INTO TROUBLE.
BACK AT THE QUEEN'S SHIP, A SAND STORM BEGINS TO PICK UP.
THIS STORM'S GOING TO SLOW THEM DOWN.
IT LOOKS PRETTY BAD.
BEEP!
PANAKA...
WE'RE RECEIVING A MESSAGE FROM HOME.
WE'LL BE RIGHT THERE.

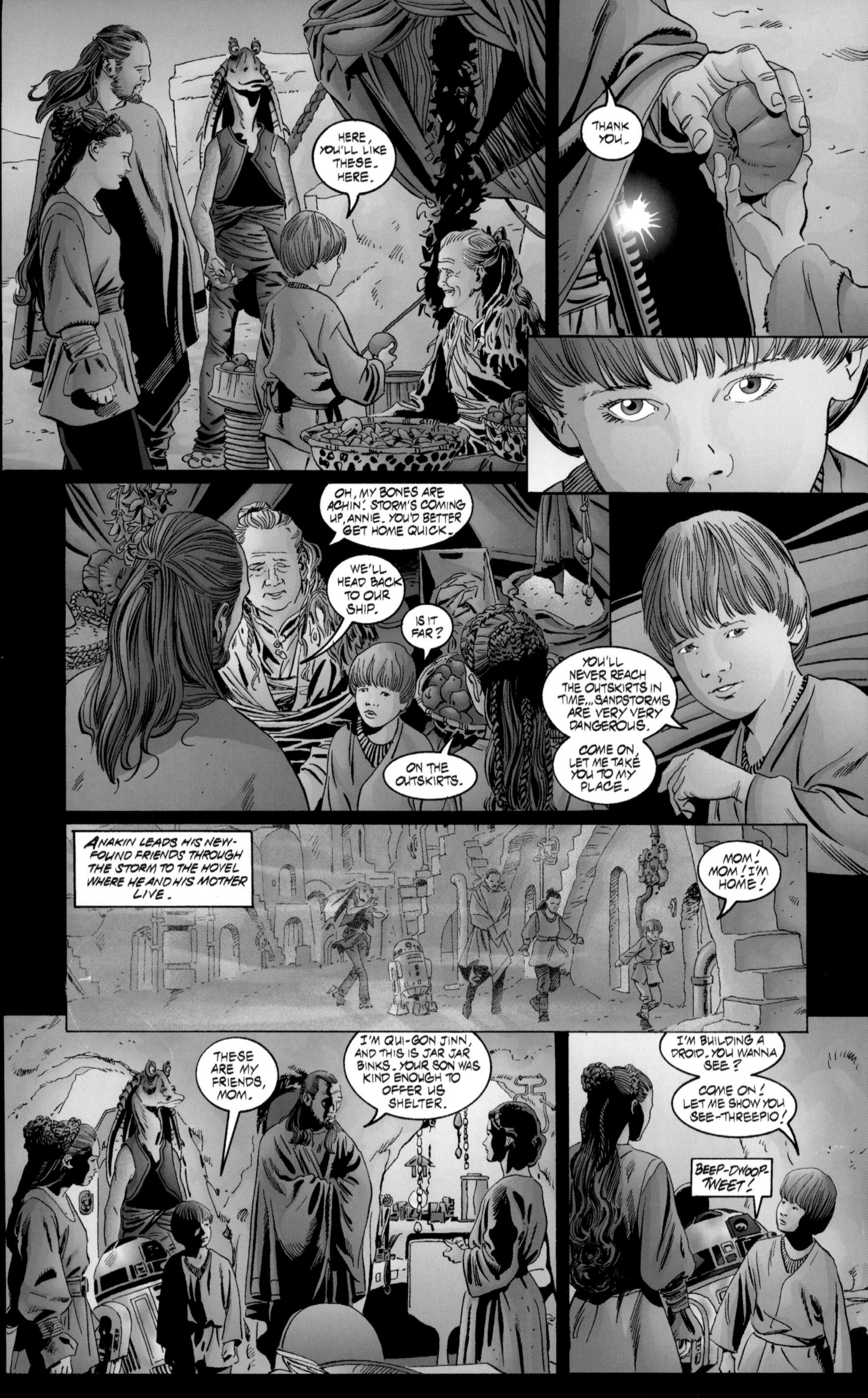
HERE, YOU'LL LIKE THESE. HERE.
THANK YOU.
OH, MY BONES ARE ACHIN'. STORM'S COMING UP, ANNIE. YOU'D BETTER GET HOME QUICK.
WE'LL HEAD BACK TO OUR SHIP.
IS IT FAR?
ON THE OUTSKIRTS.
YOU'LL NEVER REACH THE OUTSKIRTS IN TIME... SANDSTORMS ARE VERY VERY DANGEROUS.
COME ON, LET ME TAKE YOU TO MY PLACE.
ANAKIN LEADS HIS NEW-FOUND FRIENDS THROUGH THE STORM TO THE HOVEL WHERE HE AND HIS MOTHER LIVE.
MOM! MOM! I'M HOME!
THESE ARE MY FRIENDS, MOM.
I'M QUI-GON JINN, AND THIS IS JAR JAR BINKS. YOUR SON WAS KIND ENOUGH TO OFFER US SHELTER.
I'M BUILDING A DROID. YOU WANNA SEE?
COME ON! LET ME SHOW YOU SEE-THREEPIO!
BEEP-DWOOP-TWEET!

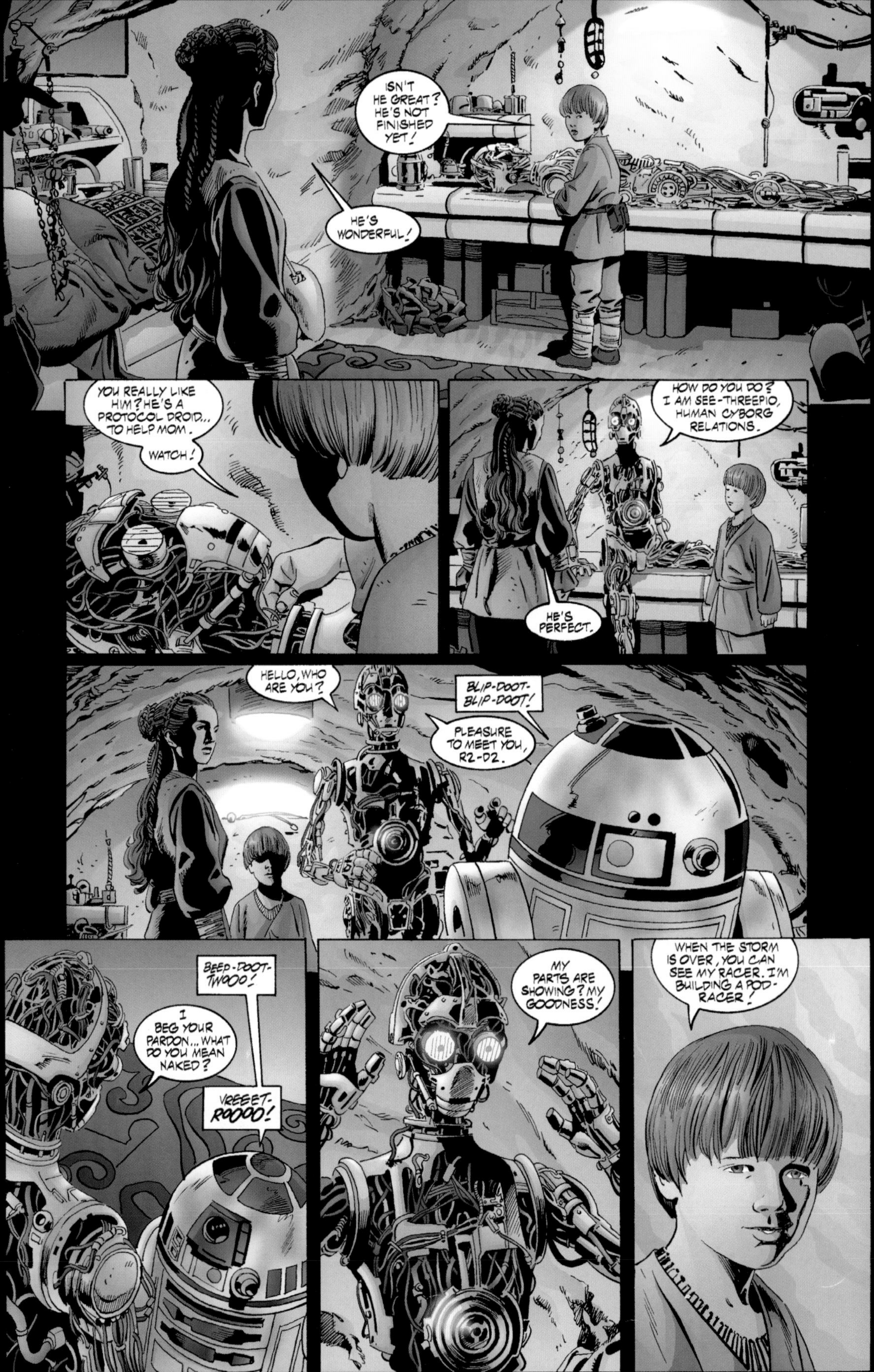
ISN'T HE GREAT? HE'S NOT FINISHED YET!
HE'S WONDERFUL!
YOU REALLY LIKE HIM? HE'S A PROTOCOL DROID... TO HELP MOM.
WATCH!
HOW DO YOU DO? I AM SEE-THREEPIO, HUMAN CYBORG RELATIONS.
HE'S PERFECT.
HELLO, WHO ARE YOU?
BLIP-DOOT-BLIP-DOOT!
PLEASURE TO MEET YOU, R2-D2.
BEEP-DOOT-TWOOO!
I BEG YOUR PARDON... WHAT DO YOU MEAN NAKED?
VREEEET-ROOOO!
MY PARTS ARE SHOWING? MY GOODNESS!
WHEN THE STORM IS OVER, YOU CAN SEE MY RACER. I'M BUILDING A POD-RACER!

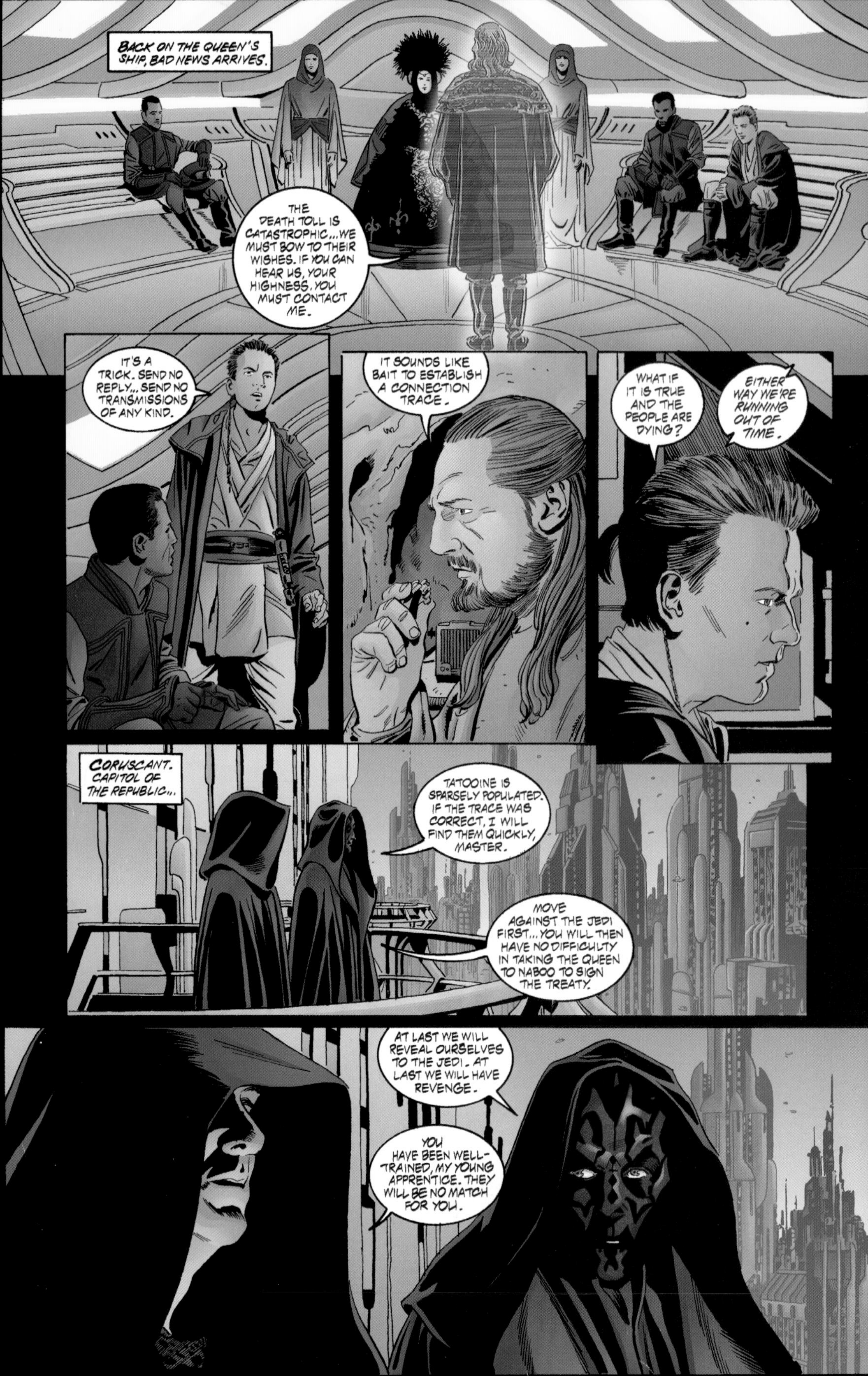
BACK ON THE QUEEN'S SHIP, BAD NEWS ARRIVES.
THE DEATH TOLL IS CATASTROPHIC... WE MUST BOW TO THEIR WISHES. IF YOU CAN HEAR US, YOUR HIGHNESS, YOU MUST CONTACT ME.
IT'S A TRICK. SEND NO REPLY... SEND NO TRANSMISSIONS OF ANY KIND.
IT SOUNDS LIKE BAIT TO ESTABLISH A CONNECTION TRACE.
WHAT IF IT IS TRUE AND THE PEOPLE ARE DYING?
EITHER WAY WE'RE RUNNING OUT OF TIME.
CORUSCANT. CAPITOL OF THE REPUBLIC...
TATOOINE IS SPARSELY POPULATED. IF THE TRACE WAS CORRECT, I WILL FIND THEM QUICKLY, MASTER.
MOVE AGAINST THE JEDI FIRST... YOU WILL THEN HAVE NO DIFFICULTY IN TAKING THE QUEEN TO NABOO TO SIGN THE TREATY.
AT LAST WE WILL REVEAL OURSELVES TO THE JEDI. AT LAST WE WILL HAVE REVENGE.
YOU HAVE BEEN WELL-TRAINED, MY YOUNG APPRENTICE. THEY WILL BE NO MATCH FOR YOU.

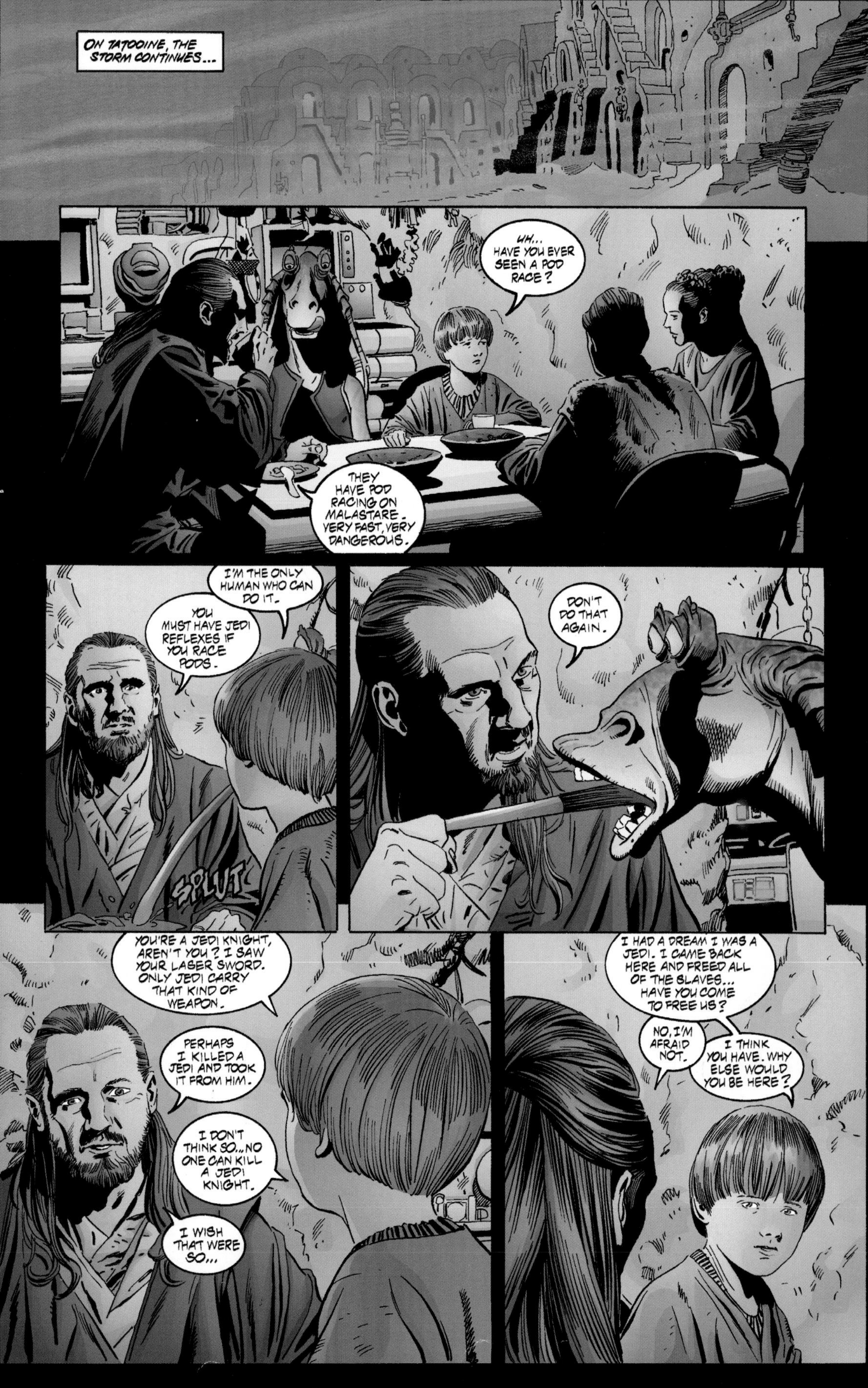
ON TATOOINE, THE STORM CONTINUES...
UH... HAVE YOU EVER SEEN A POD RACE?
THEY HAVE POD RACING ON MALASTARE. VERY FAST, VERY DANGEROUS.
I'M THE ONLY HUMAN WHO CAN DO IT.
YOU MUST HAVE JEDI REFLEXES IF YOU RACE PODS.
SPLUT
DON'T DO THAT AGAIN.
YOU'RE A JEDI KNIGHT, AREN'T YOU? I SAW YOUR LASER SWORD. ONLY JEDI CARRY THAT KIND OF WEAPON.
PERHAPS I KILLED A JEDI AND TOOK IT FROM HIM.
I DON'T THINK SO...NO ONE CAN KILL A JEDI KNIGHT.
I WISH THAT WERE SO...
I HAD A DREAM I WAS A JEDI. I CAME BACK HERE AND FREED ALL OF THE SLAVES... HAVE YOU COME TO FREE US?
NO, I'M AFRAID NOT.
I THINK YOU HAVE. WHY ELSE WOULD YOU BE HERE?

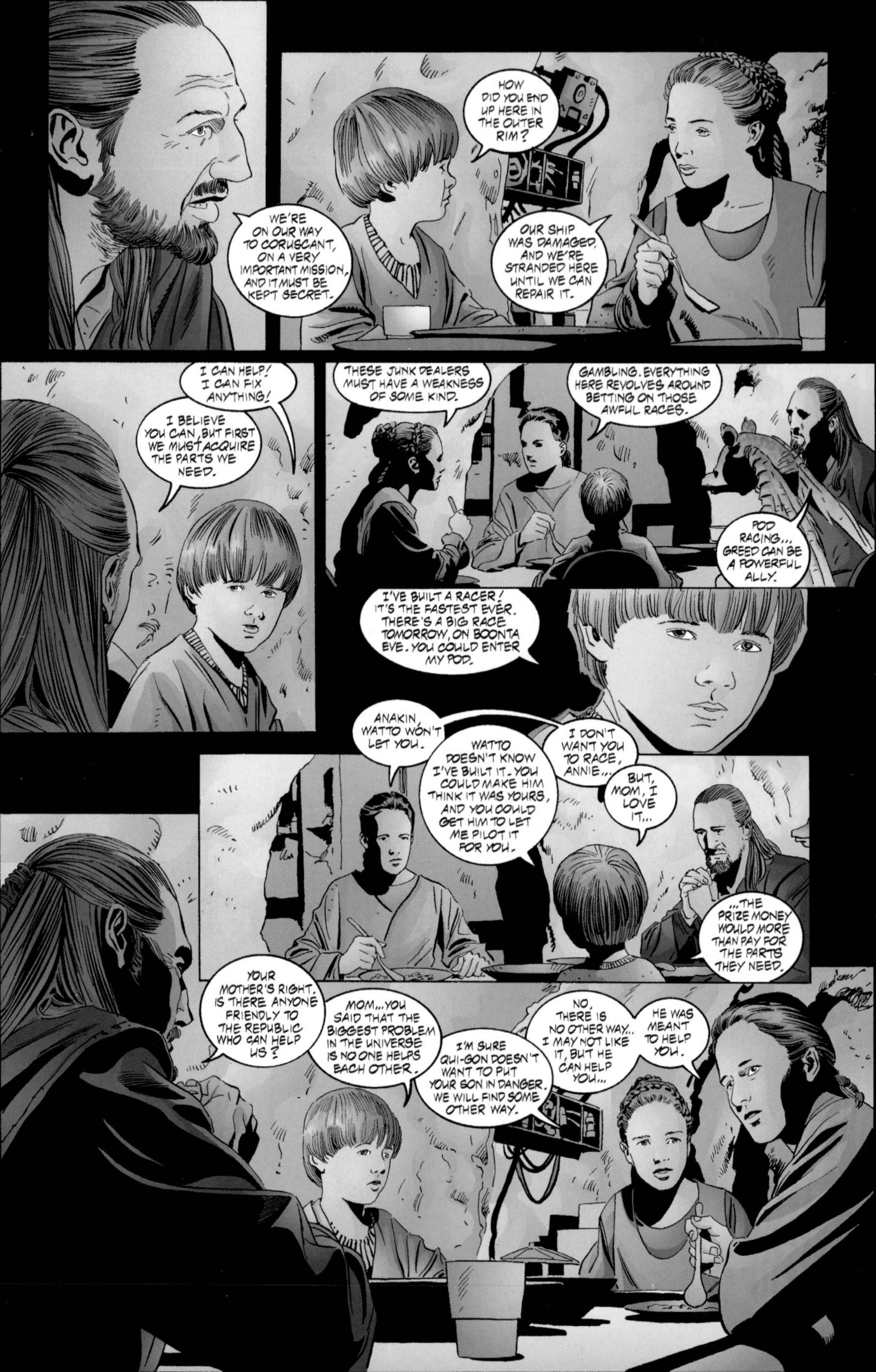
HOW DID YOU END UP HERE IN THE OUTER RIM?
WE'RE ON OUR WAY TO CORUSCANT, ON A VERY IMPORTANT MISSION, AND IT MUST BE KEPT SECRET.
OUR SHIP WAS DAMAGED, AND WE'RE STRANDED HERE UNTIL WE CAN REPAIR IT.
I CAN HELP! I CAN FIX ANYTHING!
I BELIEVE YOU CAN, BUT FIRST WE MUST ACQUIRE THE PARTS WE NEED.
THESE JUNK DEALERS MUST HAVE A WEAKNESS OF SOME KIND.
GAMBLING. EVERYTHING HERE REVOLVES AROUND BETTING ON THOSE AWFUL RACES.
POD RACING... GREED CAN BE A POWERFUL ALLY.
I'VE BUILT A RACER! IT'S THE FASTEST EVER. THERE'S A BIG RACE TOMORROW, ON BOONTA EVE. YOU COULD ENTER MY POD.
ANAKIN, WATTO WON'T LET YOU.
WATTO DOESN'T KNOW I'VE BUILT IT. YOU COULD MAKE HIM THINK IT WAS YOURS, AND YOU COULD GET HIM TO LET ME PILOT IT FOR YOU.
I DON'T WANT YOU TO RACE, ANNIE...
BUT, MOM, I LOVE IT...
...THE PRIZE MONEY WOULD MORE THAN PAY FOR THE PARTS THEY NEED.
YOUR MOTHER'S RIGHT. IS THERE ANYONE FRIENDLY TO THE REPUBLIC WHO CAN HELP US?
MOM... YOU SAID THAT THE BIGGEST PROBLEM IN THE UNIVERSE IS NO ONE HELPS EACH OTHER.
I'M SURE QUI-GON DOESN'T WANT TO PUT YOUR SON IN DANGER. WE WILL FIND SOME OTHER WAY.
NO, THERE IS NO OTHER WAY... I MAY NOT LIKE IT, BUT HE CAN HELP YOU...
HE WAS MEANT TO HELP YOU.

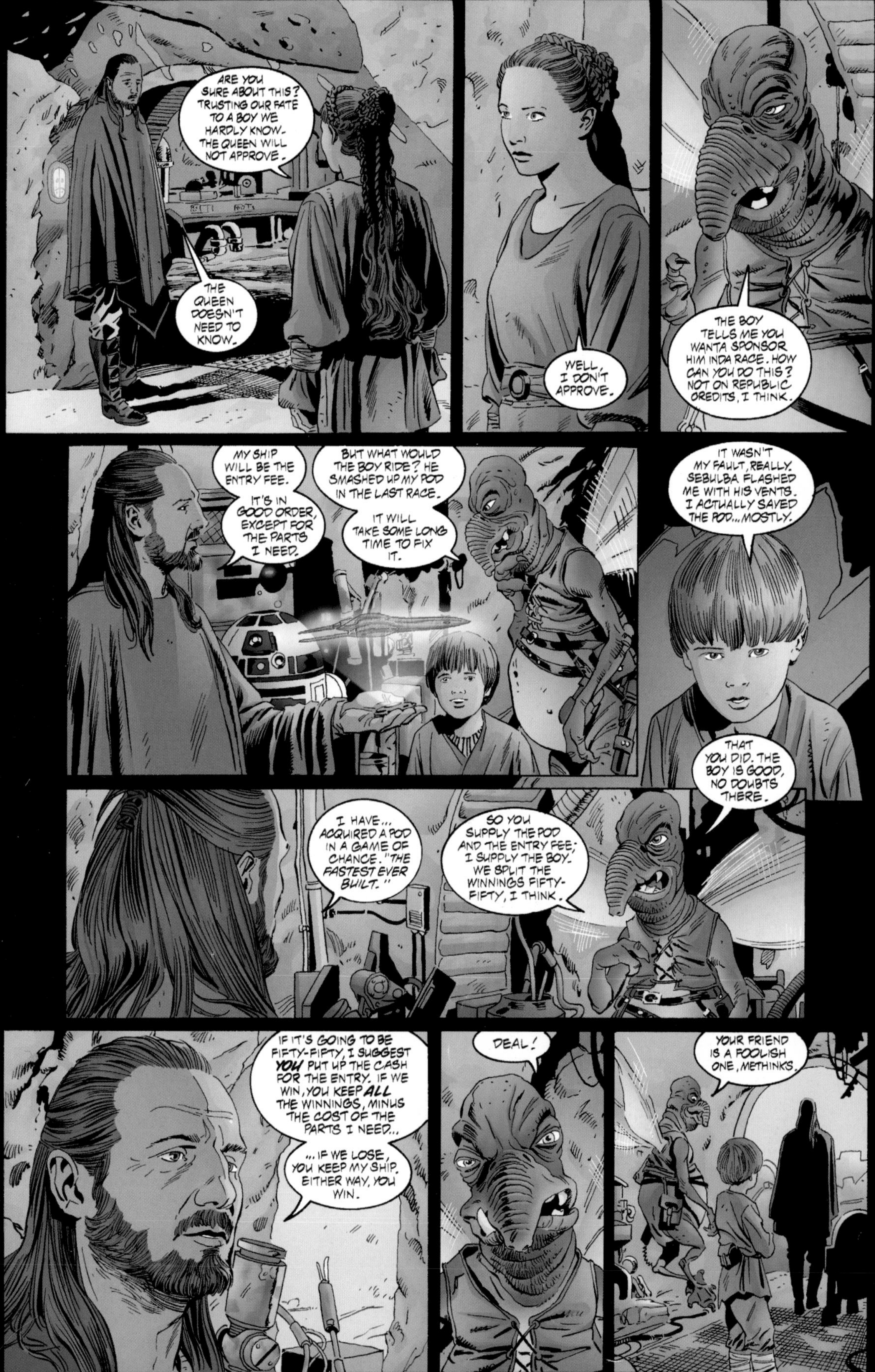
ARE YOU SURE ABOUT THIS? TRUSTING OUR FATE TO A BOY WE HARDLY KNOW. THE QUEEN WILL NOT APPROVE.
THE QUEEN DOESN'T NEED TO KNOW.
WELL, I DON'T APPROVE.
THE BOY TELLS ME YOU WANTA SPONSOR HIM INDA RACE. HOW CAN YOU DO THIS? NOT ON REPUBLIC CREDITS, I THINK.
MY SHIP WILL BE THE ENTRY FEE.
IT'S IN GOOD ORDER, EXCEPT FOR THE PARTS I NEED.
BUT WHAT WOULD THE BOY RIDE? HE SMASHED UP MY POD IN THE LAST RACE.
IT WILL TAKE SOME LONG TIME TO FIX IT.
IT WASN'T MY FAULT, REALLY. SEBULBA FLASHED ME WITH HIS VENTS. I ACTUALLY SAVED THE POD... MOSTLY.
THAT YOU DID. THE BOY IS GOOD, NO DOUBTS THERE.
I HAVE... ACQUIRED A POD IN A GAME OF CHANCE. "THE FASTEST EVER BUILT."
SO YOU SUPPLY THE POD AND THE ENTRY FEE; I SUPPLY THE BOY. WE SPLIT THE WINNINGS FIFTY-FIFTY, I THINK.
IF IT'S GOING TO BE FIFTY-FIFTY, I SUGGEST YOU PUT UP THE CASH FOR THE ENTRY. IF WE WIN, YOU KEEP ALL THE WINNINGS, MINUS THE COST OF THE PARTS I NEED...
... IF WE LOSE, YOU KEEP MY SHIP. EITHER WAY, YOU WIN.
DEAL!
YOUR FRIEND IS A FOOLISH ONE, METHINKS.

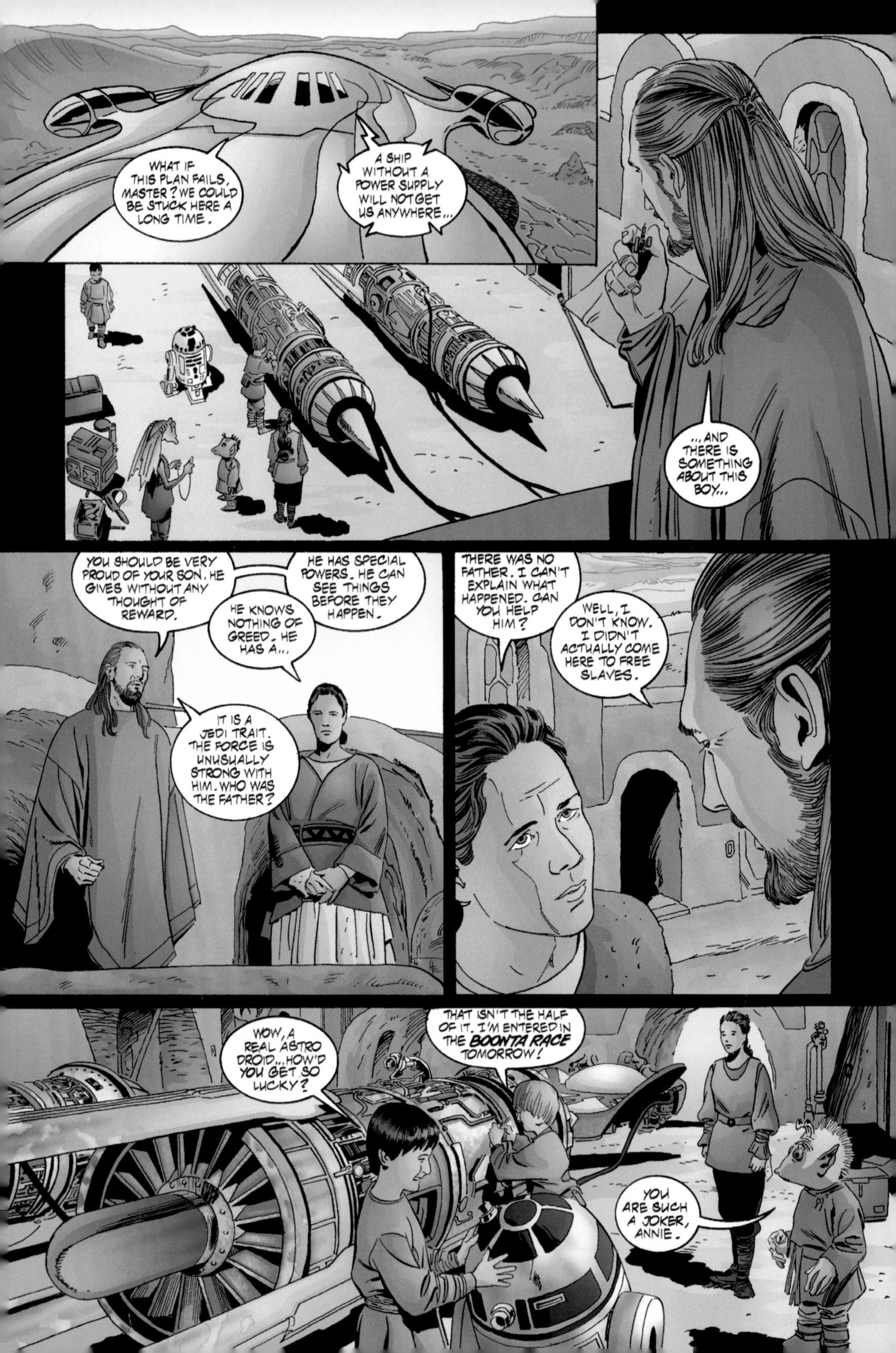

WHAT IF THIS PLAN FAILS, MASTER? WE COULD BE STUCK HERE A LONG TIME.
A SHIP WITHOUT A POWER SUPPLY WILL NOT GET US ANYWHERE...
...AND THERE IS SOMETHING ABOUT THIS BOY...
YOU SHOULD BE VERY PROUD OF YOUR SON. HE GIVES WITHOUT ANY THOUGHT OF REWARD.
HE KNOWS NOTHING OF GREED. HE HAS A...
HE HAS SPECIAL POWERS. HE CAN SEE THINGS BEFORE THEY HAPPEN.
IT IS A JEDI TRAIT. THE FORCE IS UNUSUALLY STRONG WITH HIM. WHO WAS THE FATHER?
THERE WAS NO FATHER. I CAN'T EXPLAIN WHAT HAPPENED. CAN YOU HELP HIM?
WELL, I DON'T KNOW. I DIDN'T ACTUALLY COME HERE TO FREE SLAVES.
WOW, A REAL ASTRO DROID... HOW'D YOU GET SO LUCKY?
THAT ISN'T THE HALF OF IT. I'M ENTERED IN THE BOONTA RACE TOMORROW!
YOU ARE SUCH A JOKER, ANNIE.

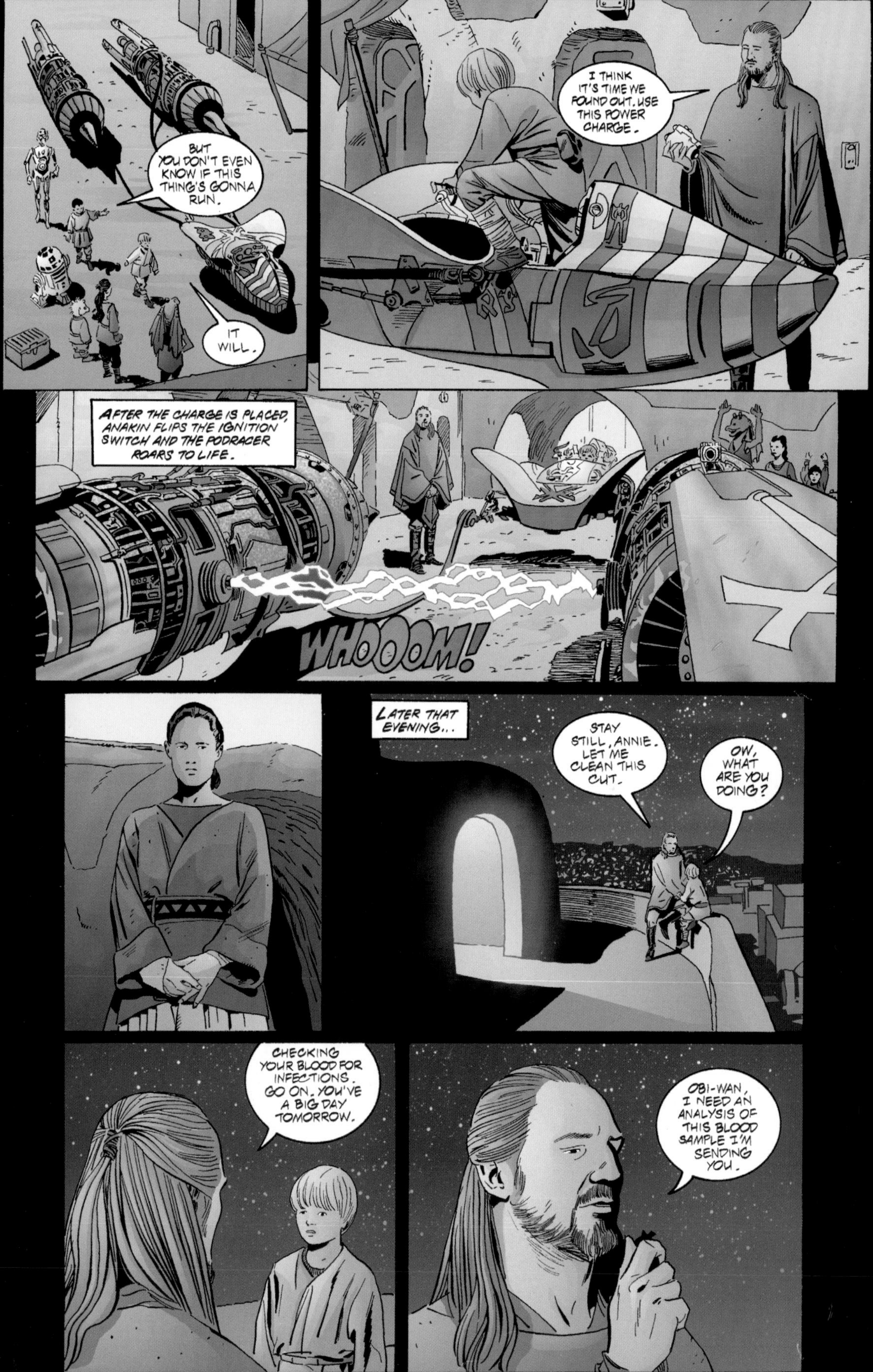
BUT YOU DON'T EVEN KNOW IF THIS THING'S GONNA RUN.
IT WILL.
I THINK IT'S TIME WE FOUND OUT. USE THIS POWER CHARGE.
AFTER THE CHARGE IS PLACED, ANAKIN FLIPS THE IGNITION SWITCH AND THE PODRACER ROARS TO LIFE.
WHOOOM!
LATER THAT EVENING...
STAY STILL, ANNIE. LET ME CLEAN THIS CUT.
OW, WHAT ARE YOU DOING?
CHECKING YOUR BLOOD FOR INFECTIONS. GO ON. YOU'VE A BIG DAY TOMORROW.
OBI-WAN, I NEED AN ANALYSIS OF THIS BLOOD SAMPLE I'M SENDING YOU.

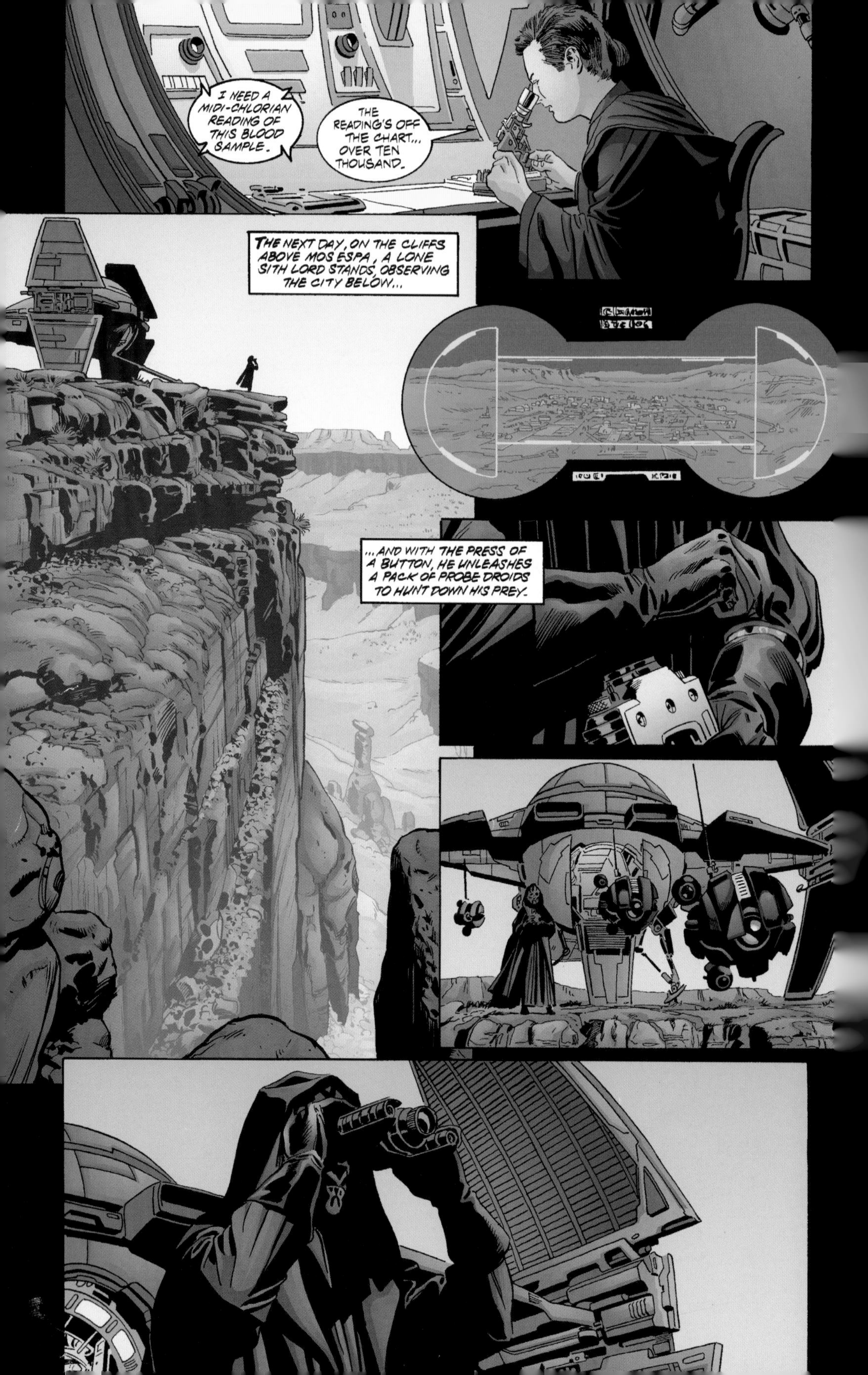
I NEED A MIDI-CHLORIAN READING OF THIS BLOOD SAMPLE.
THE READING'S OFF THE CHART... OVER TEN THOUSAND.
THE NEXT DAY, ON THE CLIFFS ABOVE MOS ESPA, A LONE SITH LORD STANDS, OBSERVING THE CITY BELOW...
...AND WITH THE PRESS OF A BUTTON, HE UNLEASHES A PACK OF PROBE DROIDS TO HUNT DOWN HIS PREY.

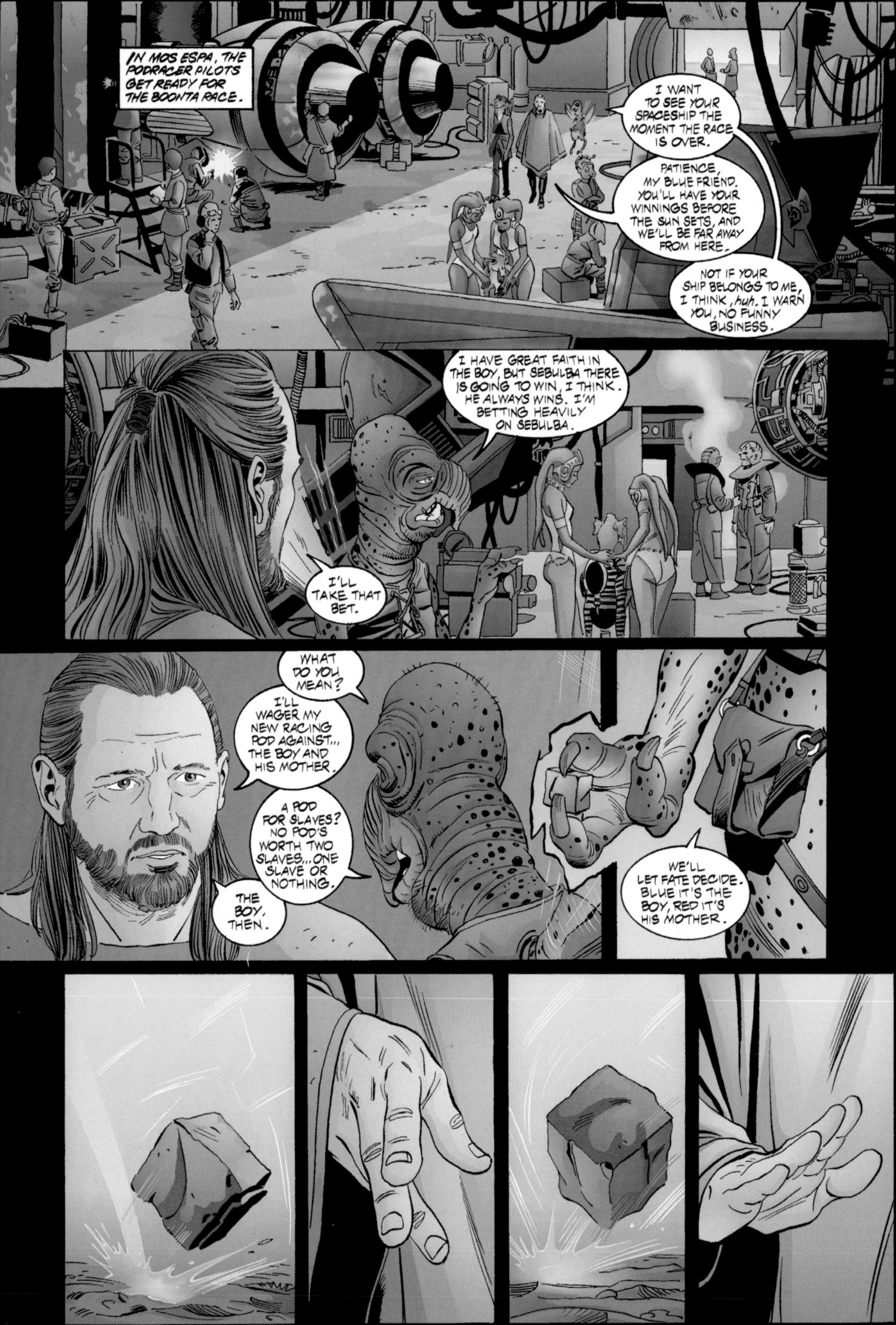
IN MOS ESPA, THE PODRACER PILOTS GET READY FOR THE BOONTA RACE.
I WANT TO SEE YOUR SPACESHIP THE MOMENT THE RACE IS OVER.
PATIENCE, MY BLUE FRIEND. YOU'LL HAVE YOUR WINNINGS BEFORE THE SUN SETS, AND WE'LL BE FAR AWAY FROM HERE.
NOT IF YOUR SHIP BELONGS TO ME, I THINK, huh. I WARN YOU, NO FUNNY BUSINESS.
I HAVE GREAT FAITH IN THE BOY, BUT SEBULBA THERE IS GOING TO WIN, I THINK. HE ALWAYS WINS. I'M BETTING HEAVILY ON SEBULBA.
I'LL TAKE THAT BET.
WHAT DO YOU MEAN?
I'LL WAGER MY NEW RACING POD AGAINST... THE BOY AND HIS MOTHER.
A POD FOR SLAVES? NO POD'S WORTH TWO SLAVES... ONE SLAVE OR NOTHING.
THE BOY, THEN.
WE'LL LET FATE DECIDE. BLUE IT'S THE BOY, RED IT'S HIS MOTHER.

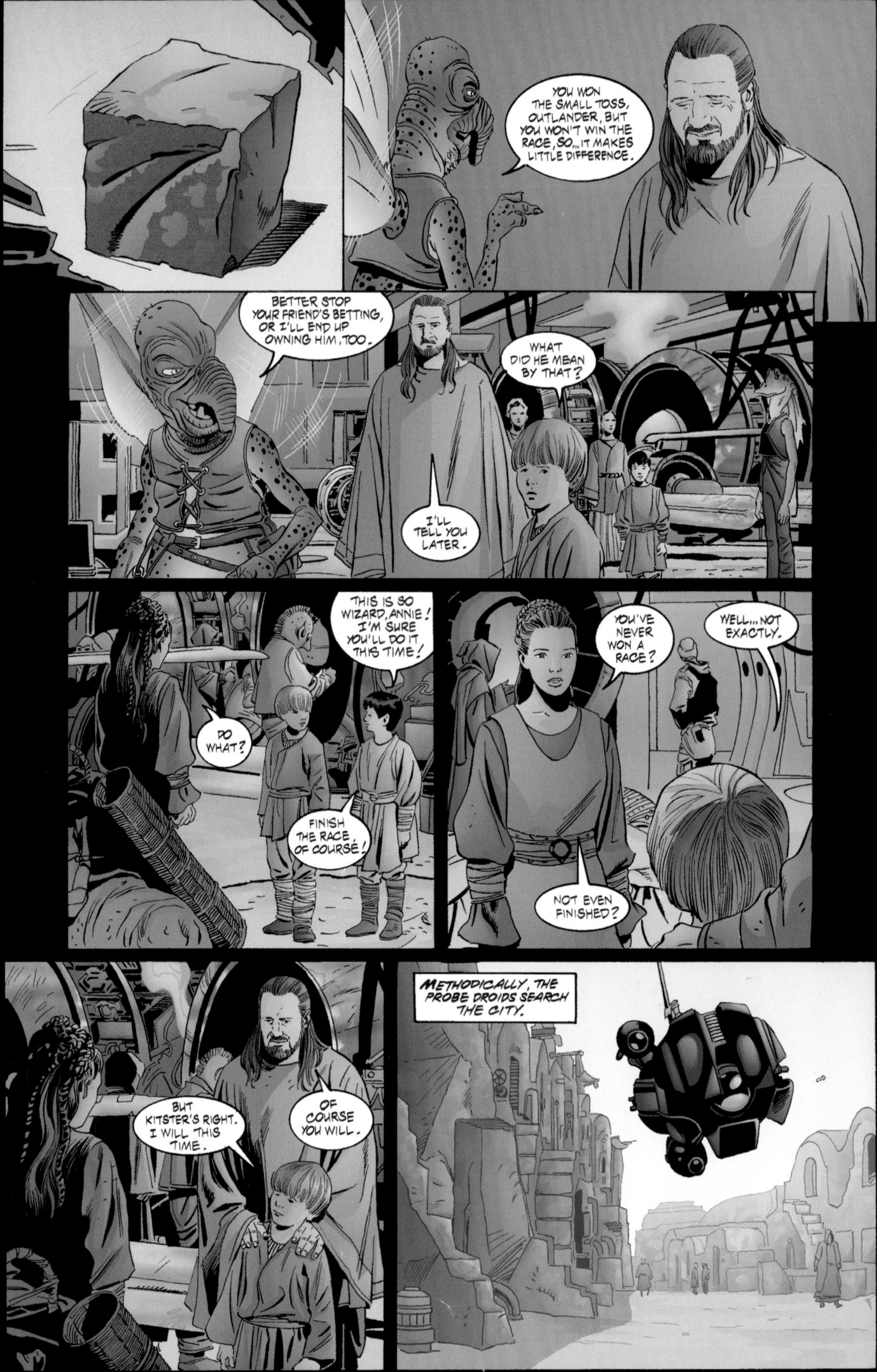
YOU WON THE SMALL TOSS, OUTLANDER, BUT YOU WON'T WIN THE RACE, SO... IT MAKES LITTLE DIFFERENCE.
BETTER STOP YOUR FRIEND'S BETTING, OR I'LL END UP OWNING HIM, TOO.
WHAT DID HE MEAN BY THAT?
I'LL TELL YOU LATER.
THIS IS SO WIZARD, ANNIE! I'M SURE YOU'LL DO IT THIS TIME!
DO WHAT?
FINISH THE RACE, OF COURSE!
YOU'VE NEVER WON A RACE?
WELL... NOT EXACTLY.
NOT EVEN FINISHED?
BUT KITSTER'S RIGHT. I WILL THIS TIME.
OF COURSE YOU WILL.
METHODICALLY, THE PROBE DROIDS SEARCH THE CITY.

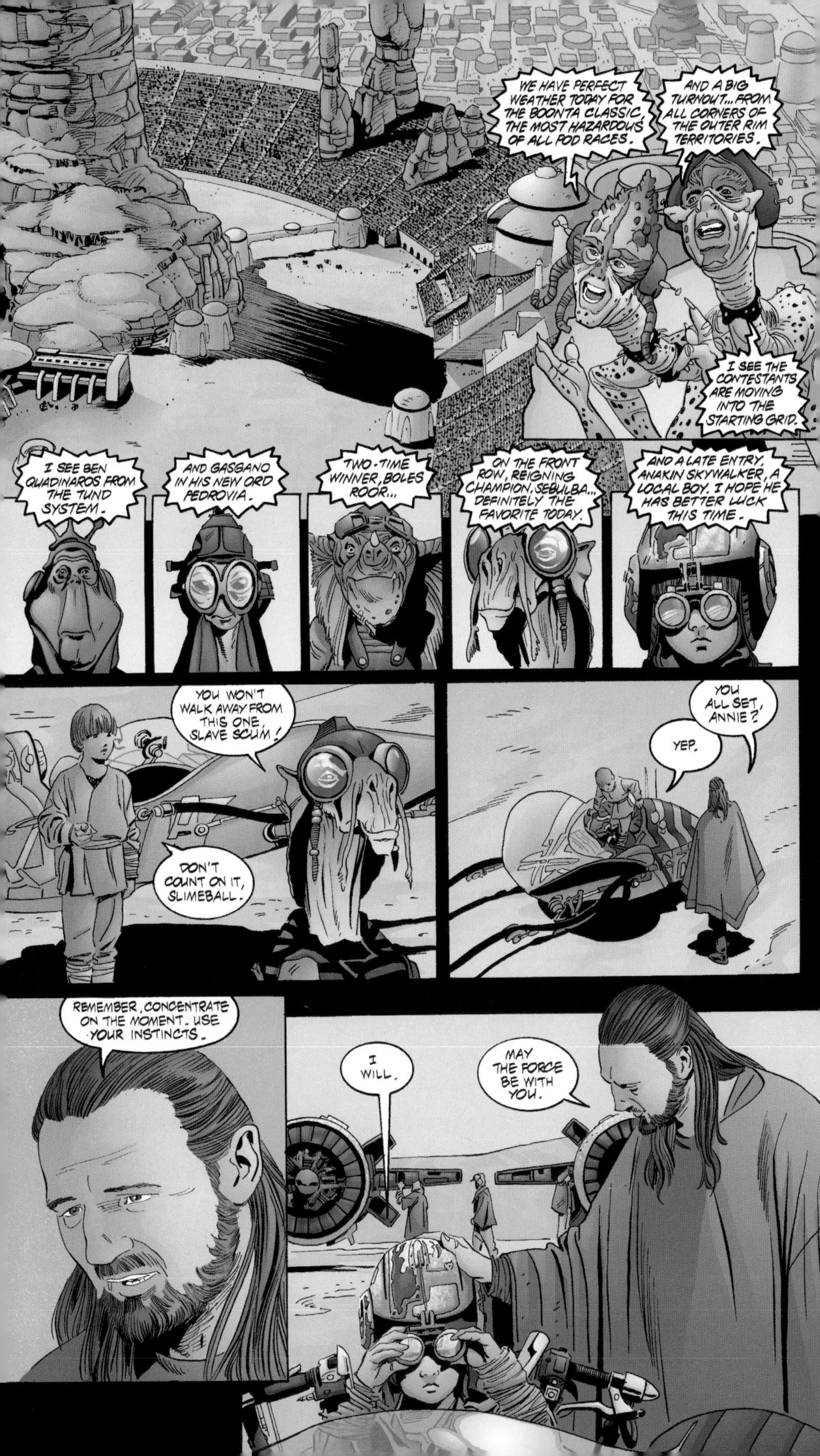
WE HAVE PERFECT WEATHER TODAY FOR THE BOONTA CLASSIC, THE MOST HAZARDOUS OF ALL POD RACES.
AND A BIG TURNOUT... FROM ALL CORNERS OF THE OUTER RIM TERRITORIES.
I SEE THE CONTESTANTS ARE MOVING INTO THE STARTING GRID.
I SEE BEN QUADINAROS FROM THE TUND SYSTEM.
AND GASGANO IN HIS NEW ORD PEDROVIA.
TWO-TIME WINNER, BOLES ROOR...
ON THE FRONT ROW, REIGNING CHAMPION, SEBULBA... DEFINITELY THE FAVORITE TODAY.
AND A LATE ENTRY, ANAKIN SKYWALKER, A LOCAL BOY. I HOPE HE HAS BETTER LUCK THIS TIME.
YOU WON'T WALK AWAY FROM THIS ONE, SLAVE SCUM!
DON'T COUNT ON IT, SLIMEBALL.
YOU ALL SET, ANNIE?
YEP.
REMEMBER, CONCENTRATE ON THE MOMENT. USE YOUR INSTINCTS.
I WILL.
MAY THE FORCE BE WITH YOU.

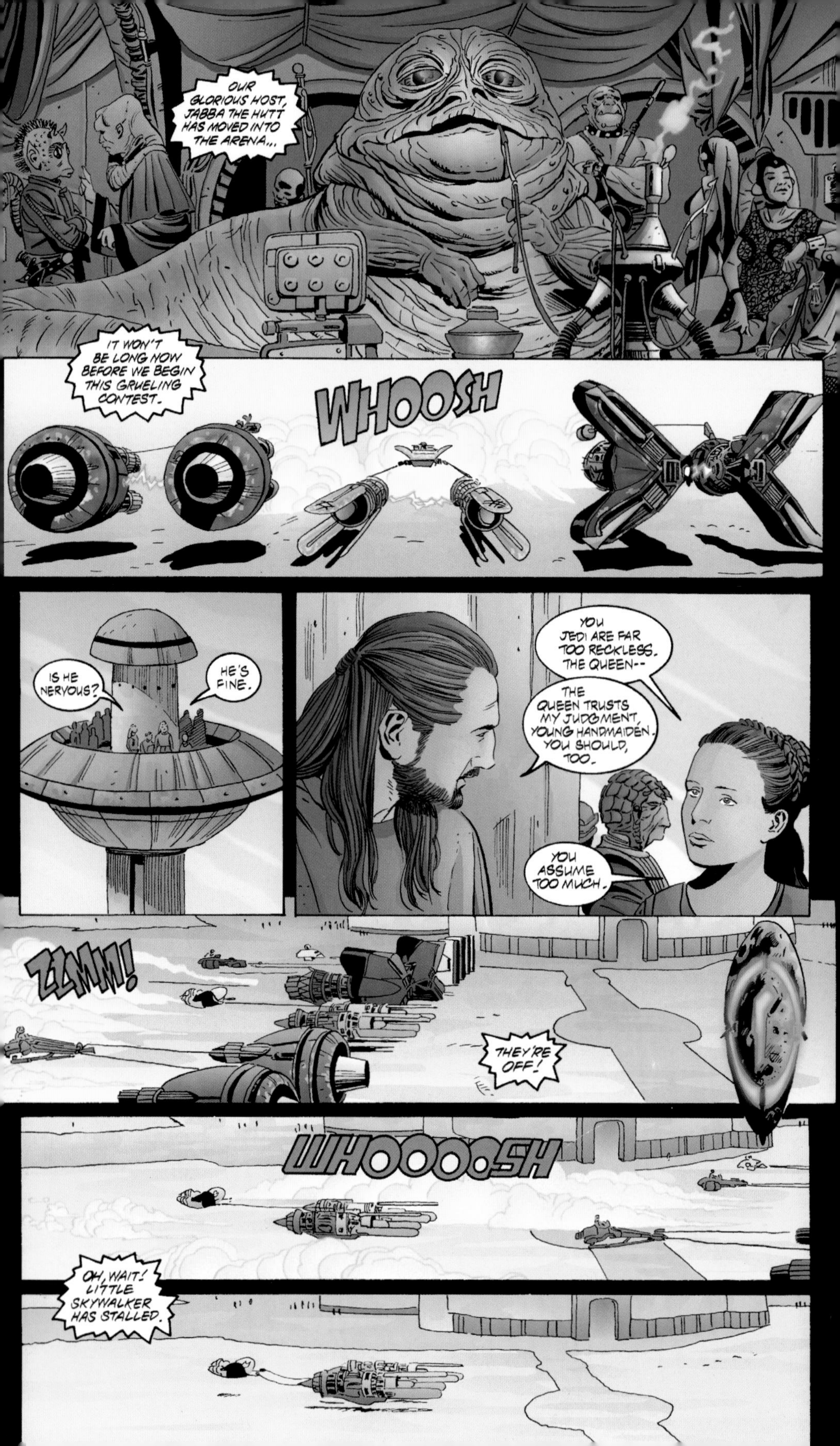
OUR GLORIOUS HOST, JABBA THE HUTT HAS MOVED INTO THE ARENA...
IT WON'T BE LONG NOW BEFORE WE BEGIN THIS GRUELING CONTEST.
WHOOSH
IS HE NERVOUS?
HE'S FINE.
YOU JEDI ARE FAR TOO RECKLESS. THE QUEEN--
THE QUEEN TRUSTS MY JUDGMENT, YOUNG HANDMAIDEN. YOU SHOULD, TOO.
YOU ASSUME TOO MUCH.
ZZMMM!
THEY'RE OFF!
WHOOOOSH
OH, WAIT! LITTLE SKYWALKER HAS STALLED.

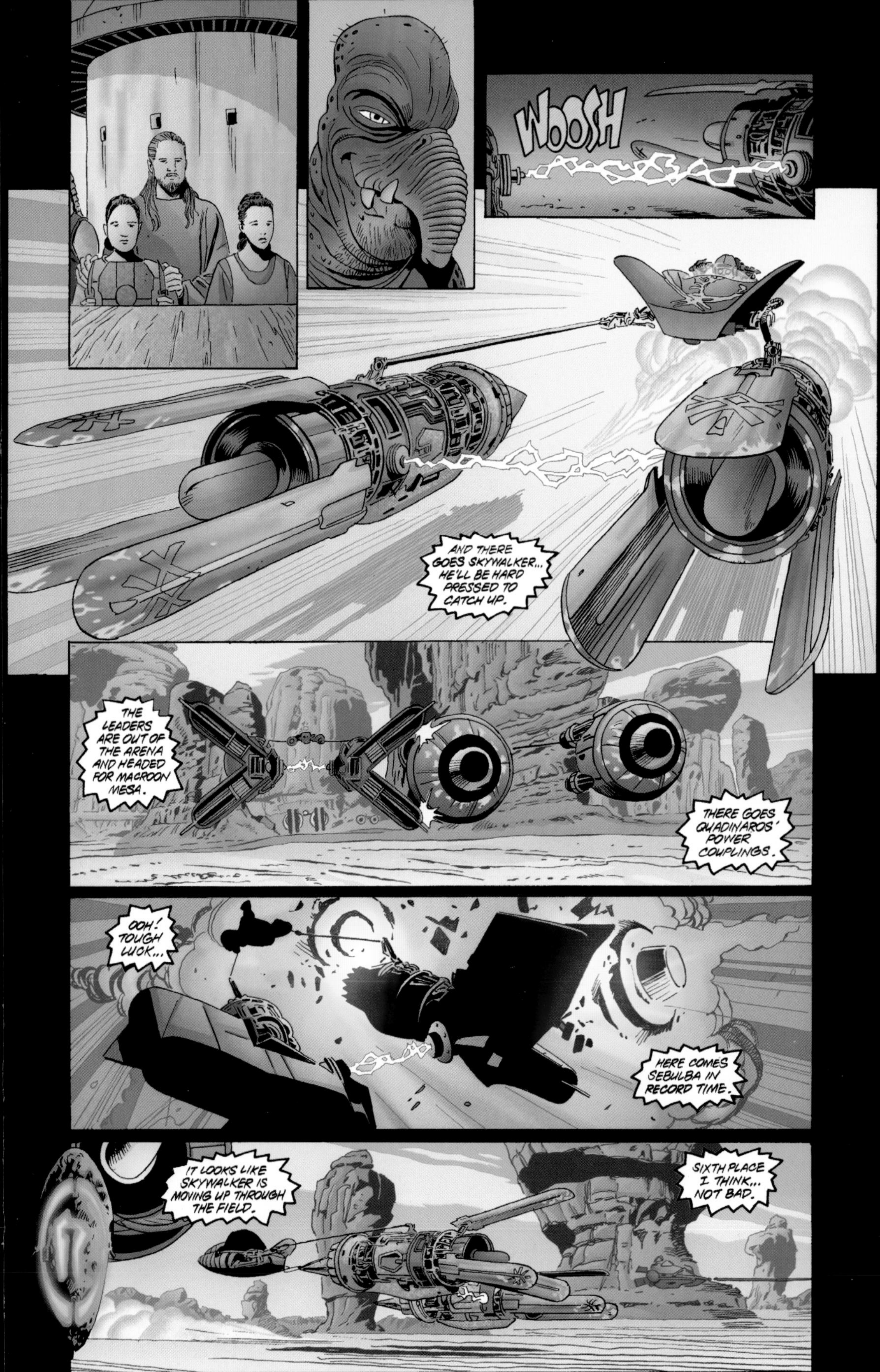
WOOSH
AND THERE GOES SKYWALKER... HE'LL BE HARD PRESSED TO CATCH UP.
THE LEADERS ARE OUT OF THE ARENA AND HEADED FOR MACROON MESA.
THERE GOES QUADINAROS' POWER COUPLINGS.
OOH! TOUGH LUCK...
HERE COMES SEBULBA IN RECORD TIME.
IT LOOKS LIKE SKYWALKER IS MOVING UP THROUGH THE FIELD.
SIXTH PLACE I THINK... NOT BAD.

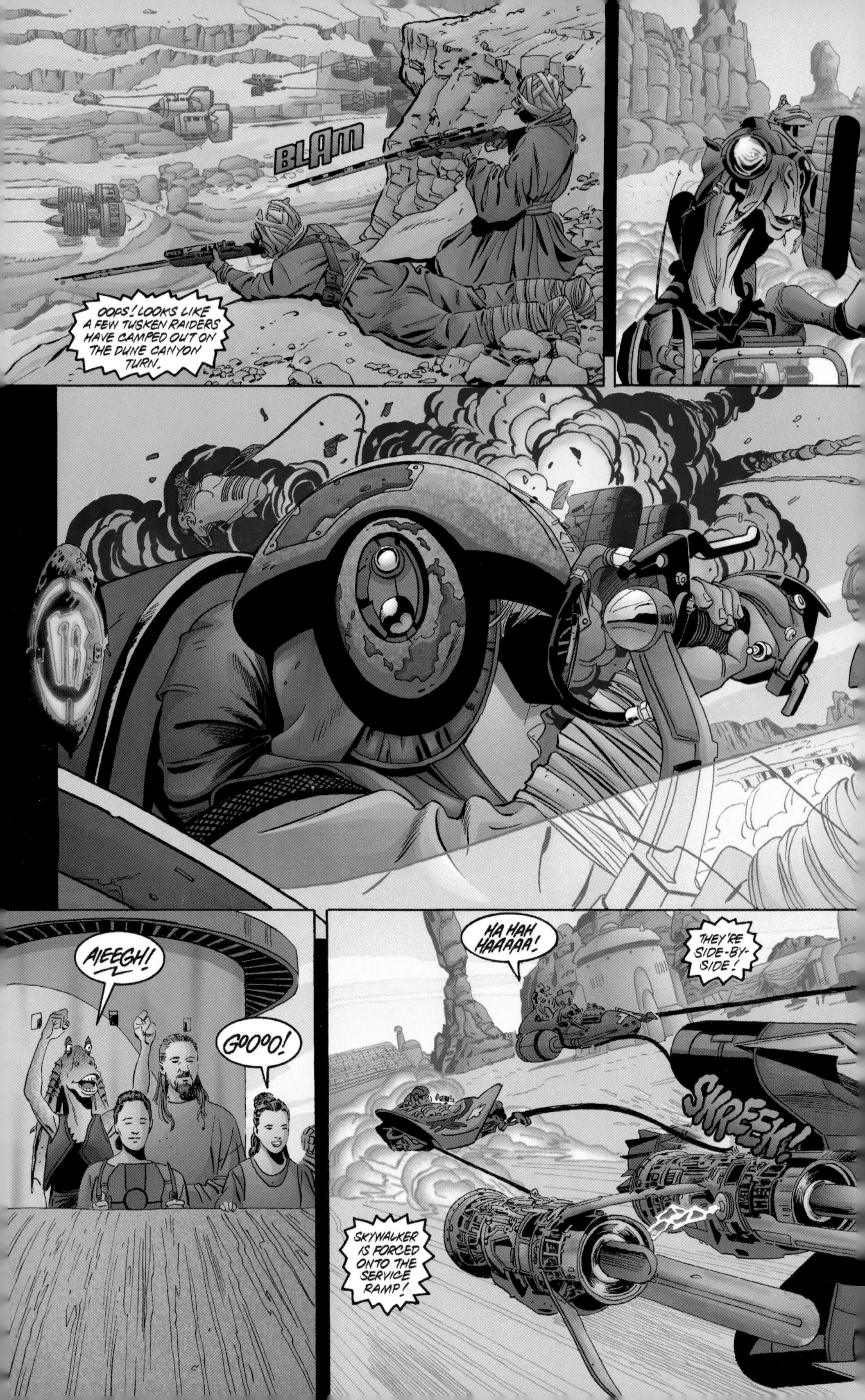
BLAM
OOPS! LOOKS LIKE A FEW TUSKEN RAIDERS HAVE CAMPED OUT ON THE DUNE CANYON TURN.
AIEEGH!
GOOOO!
HA HAH HAAAAA!
THEY'RE SIDE-BY-SIDE!
SKREEK!
SKYWALKER IS FORCED ONTO THE SERVICE RAMP!

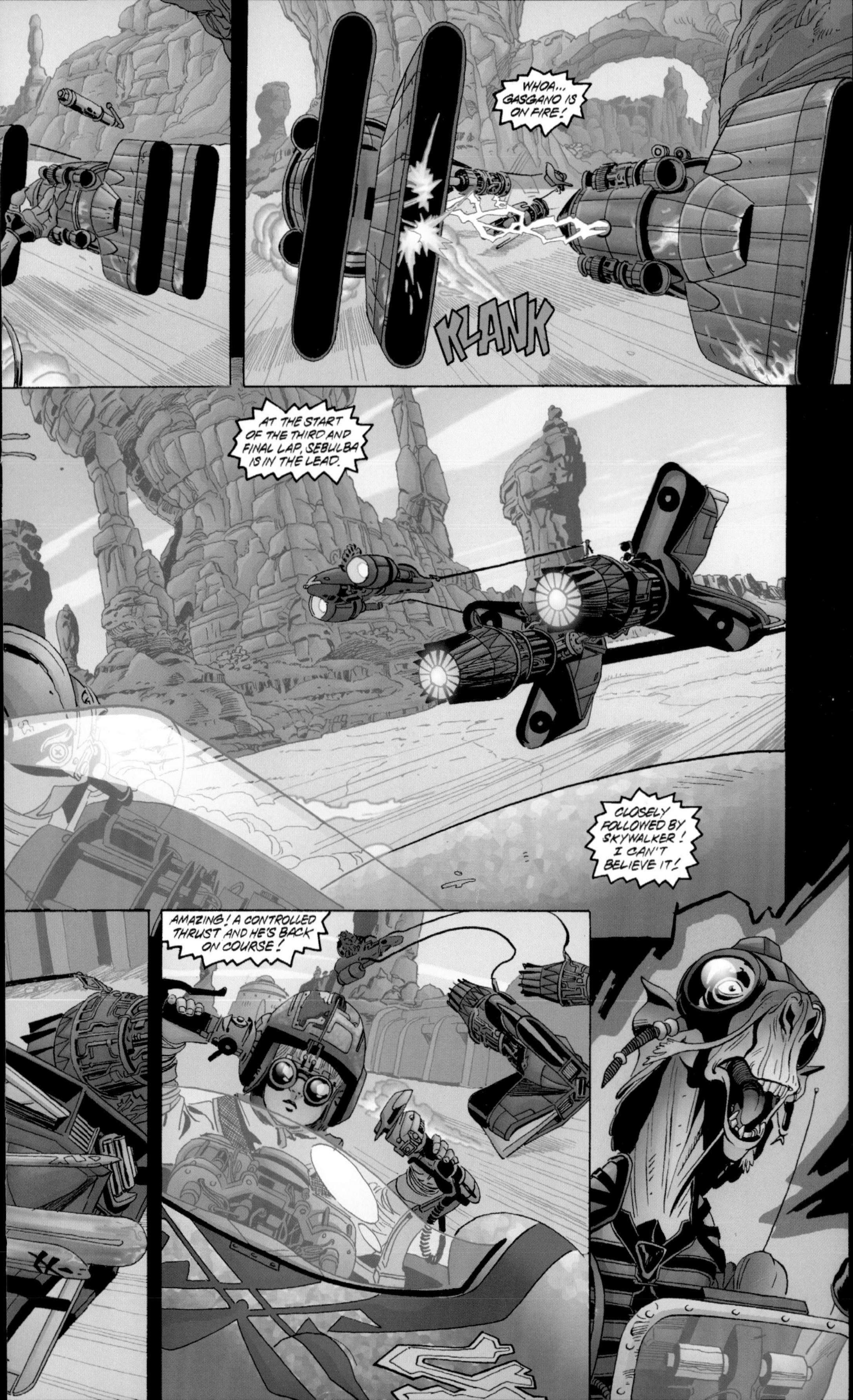
WHOA... GASGANO IS ON FIRE!
KLANK
AT THE START OF THE THIRD AND FINAL LAP, SEBULBA IS IN THE LEAD.
CLOSELY FOLLOWED BY SKYWALKER! I CAN'T BELIEVE IT!
AMAZING! A CONTROLLED THRUST AND HE'S BACK ON COURSE!

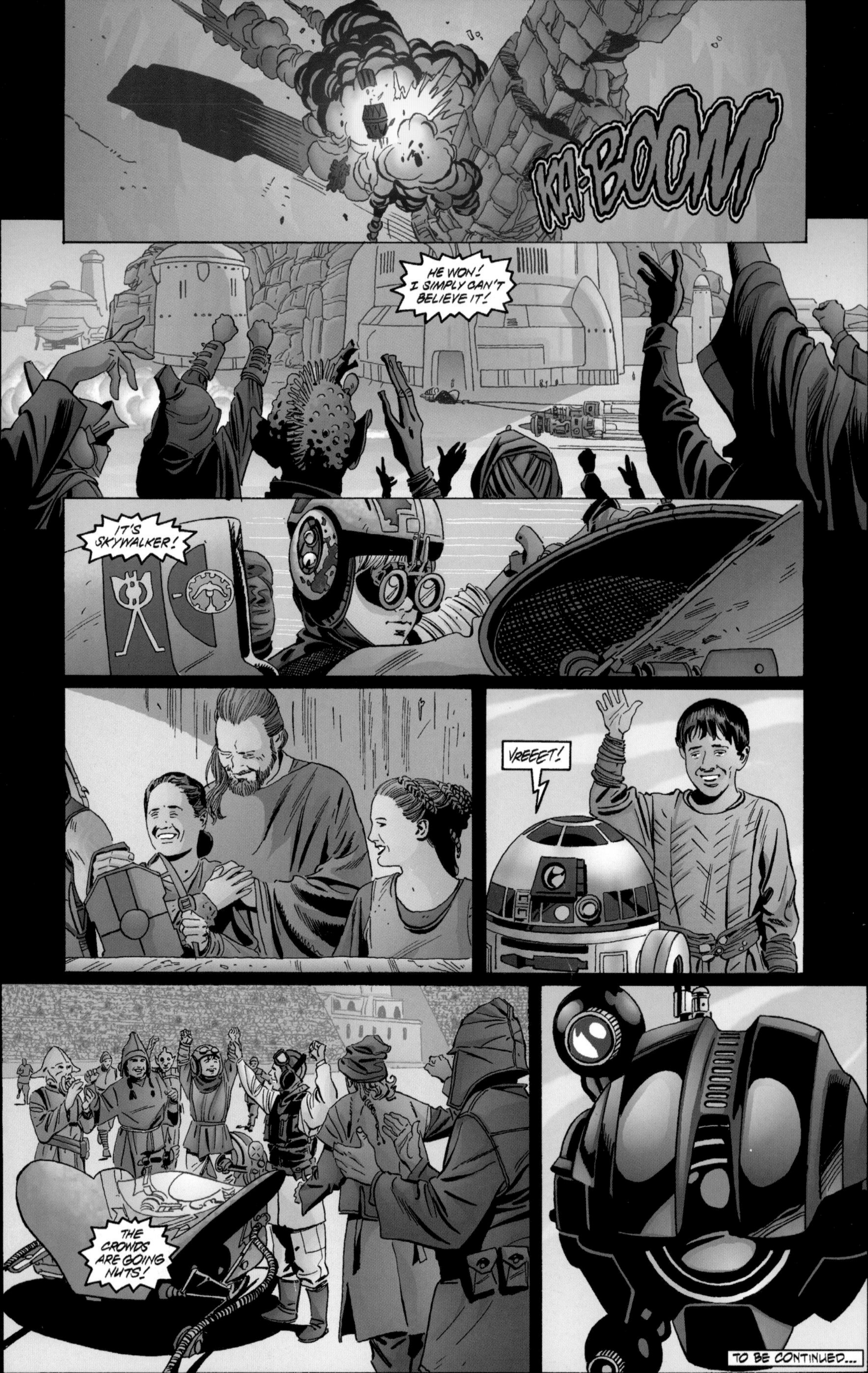
KA-BOOM
HE WON! I SIMPLY CAN'T BELIEVE IT!
IT'S SKYWALKER!
VREEET!
THE CROWDS ARE GOING NUTS!
TO BE CONTINUED...

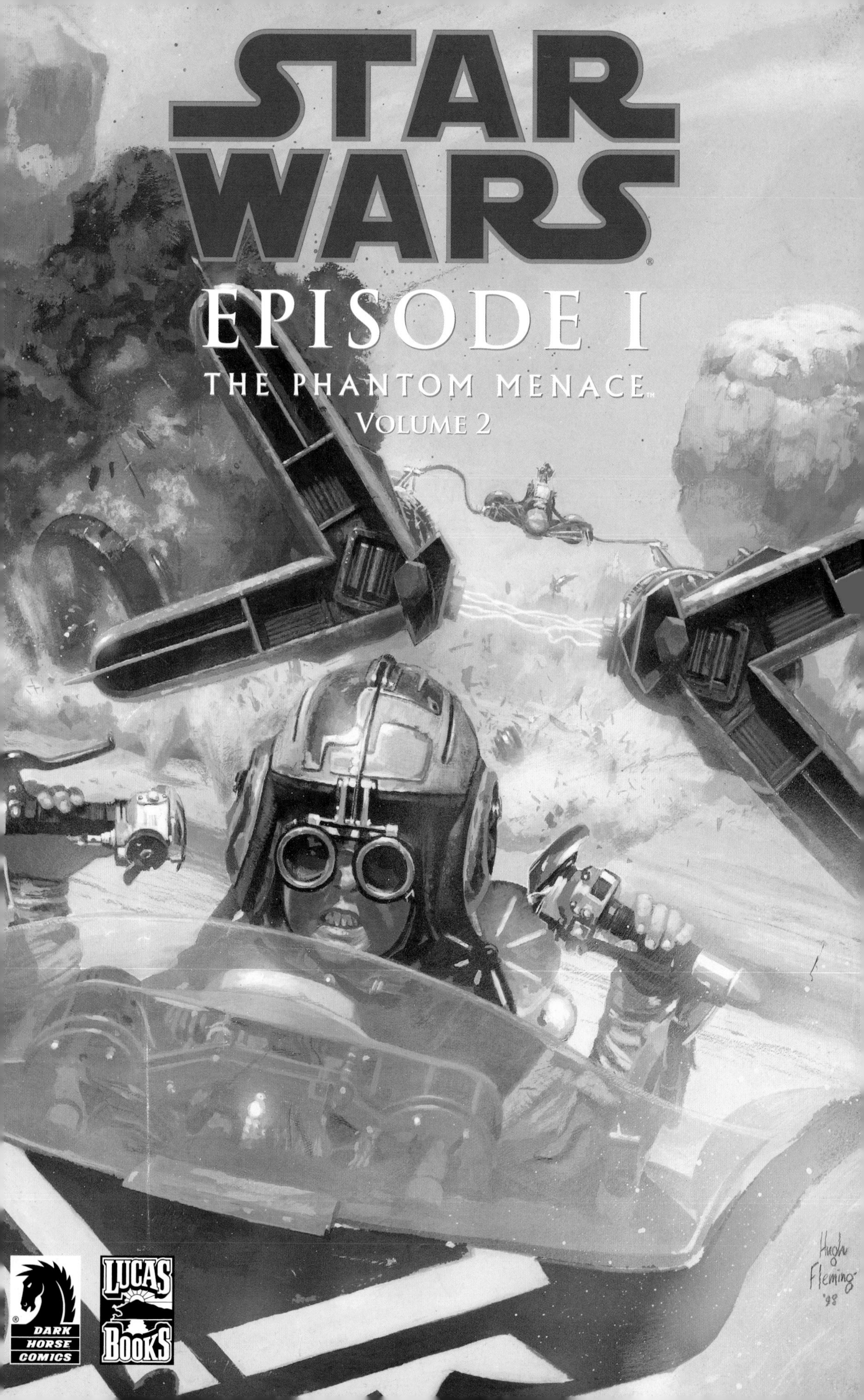
STAR WARS®
EPISODE I
THE PHANTOM MENACE™
VOLUME 2
DARK HORSE COMICS
LUCAS BOOKS
Hugh Fleming '98

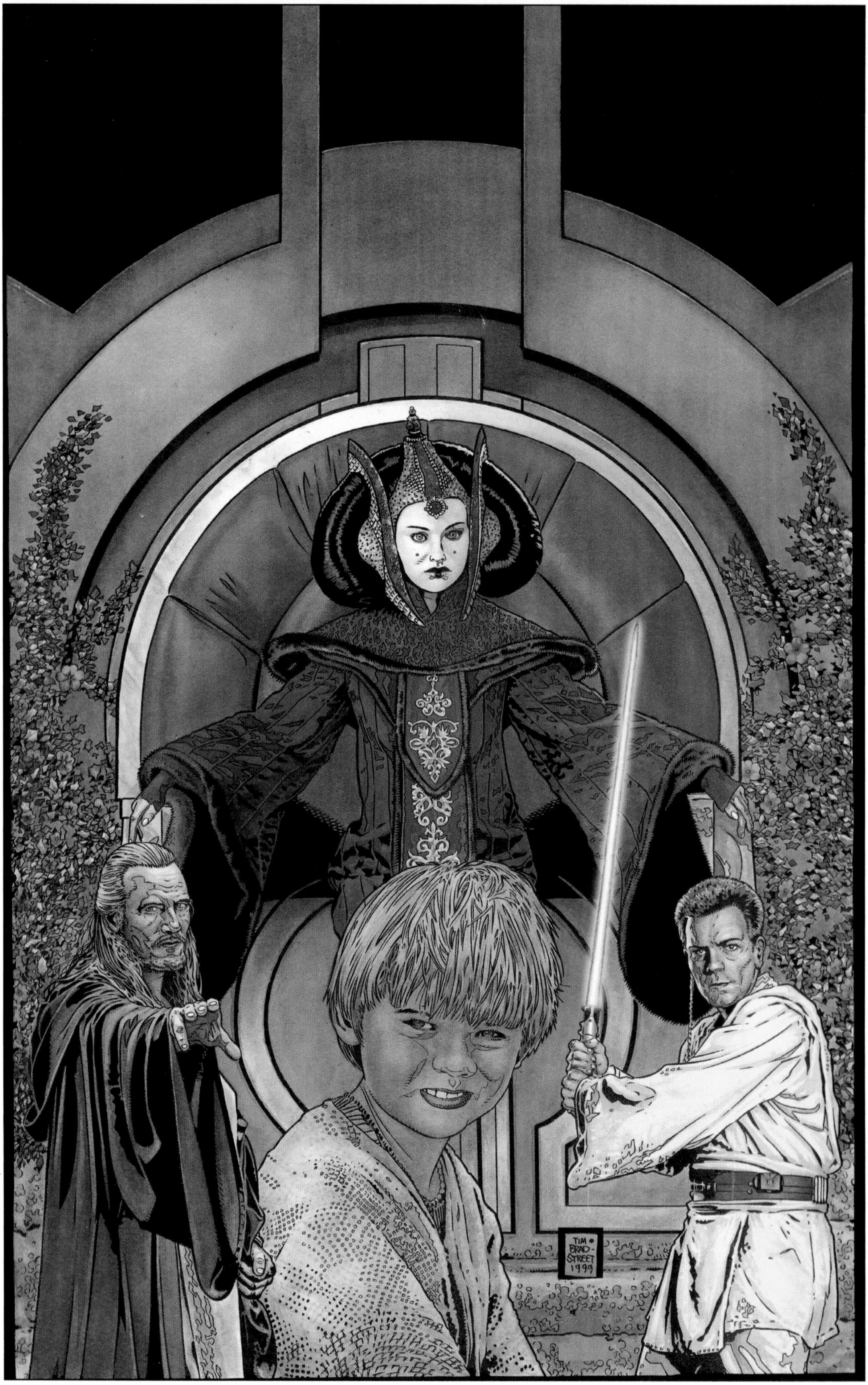
TIM
BRAD-
STREET
1999

ART BY **TIM BRADSTREET**

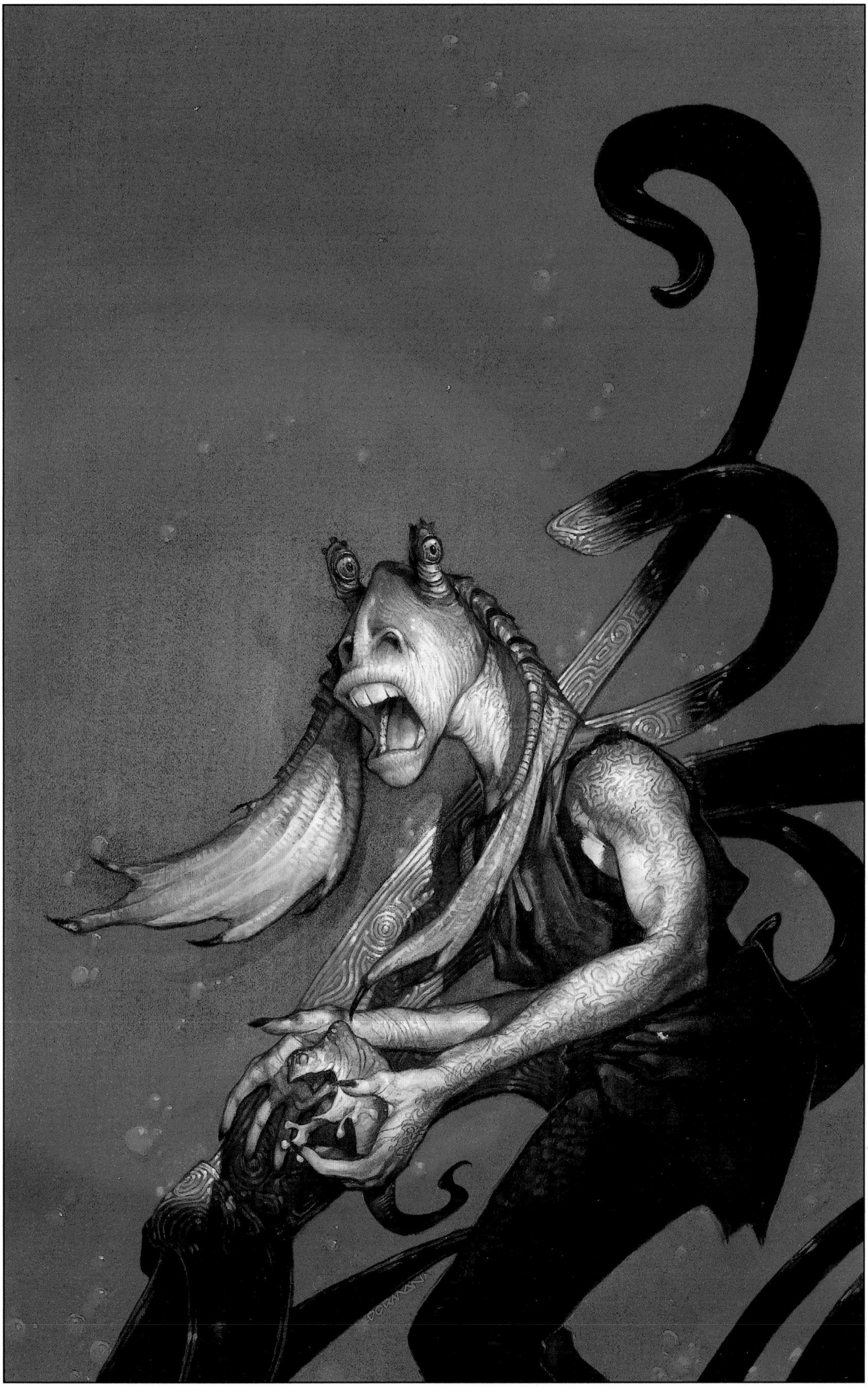

ART BY **DAVE DORMAN**

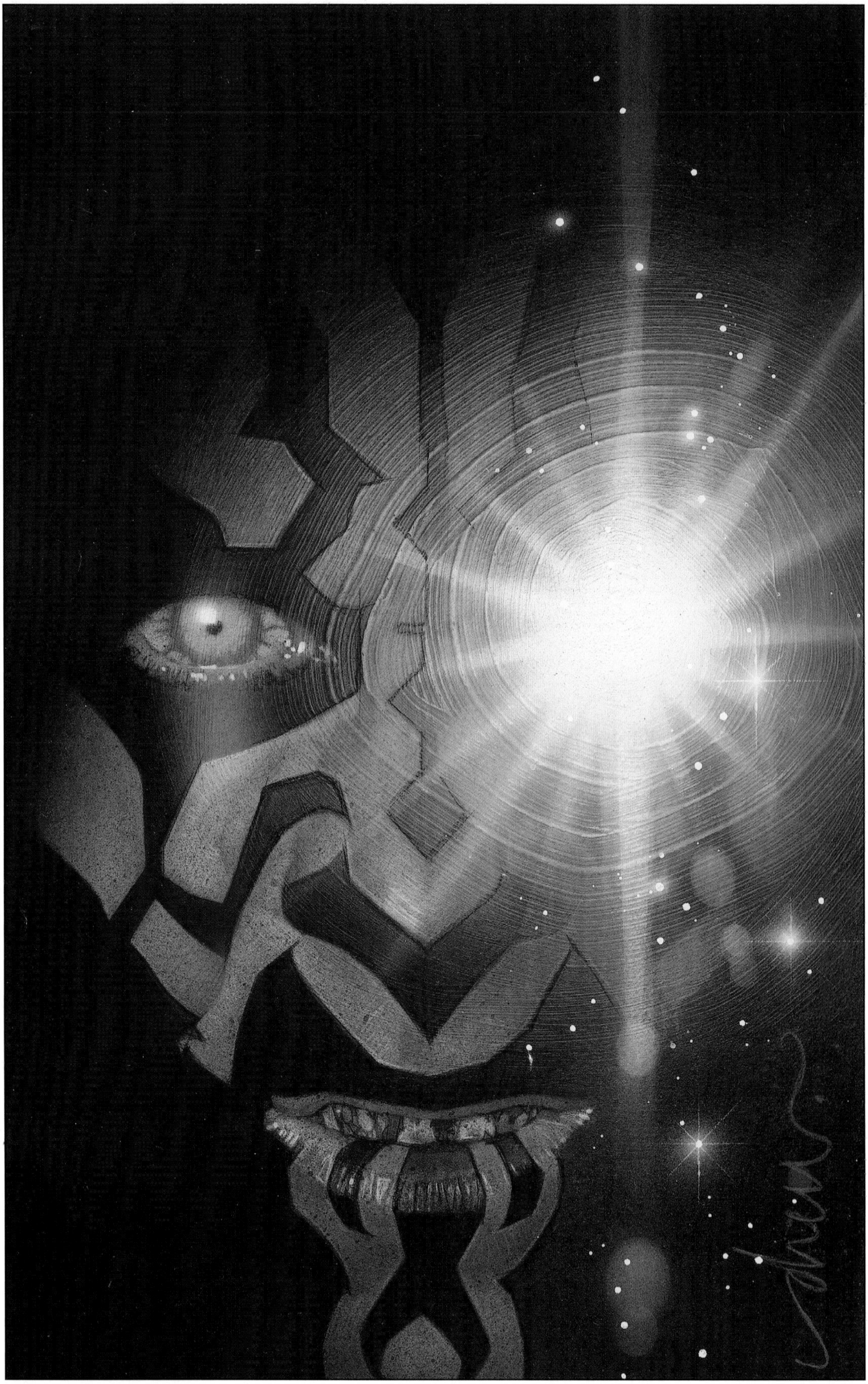

ART BY **DREW STRUZAN**